The Millionth Year

A. M. Huff

CONTENTS

DEDICATION

This novel is dedicated to the memory of my uncle,
my counselor, my friend,
Craig Saunders McCracken,
who was never afraid to be himself,
no matter what others thought.
"If they can't handle it, that is their problem, not
yours."

ACKNOWLEDGMENTS

Special thanks to Laurie Christenson for her invaluable critique and editing assistance; to Pam Bainbridge-Cowan, and Lisa Cromwell, for their time and encouragement. It truly means a lot.

CHAPTER ONE

How did I let things get so out of control?

Cory Martin turned the collar of his sport coat up against the pouring rain while he stood on the sidewalk across from La Stazione Italian Restaurant. His short chestnut hair looked three shades darker soaking wet and dripped down the back of his neck.. He cringed. Squinting up at the dark afternoon sky he searched for any sign that the rain would let up. No luck.

Why didn't I grab my raincoat instead? he cursed himself. *To be fair, the weatherman did say there was only a slight chance of rain.*

"A slight chance," he grumbled and shook his head sending more droplets down his back. He should have known better from growing up in Oregon. There a slight chance of rain meant rain; but he wasn't in Oregon and hadn't been for ten years. He was living in a condo in San Francisco. He silenced the voices in his head, and hurried across the street.

"Good afternoon, Mister Martin," greeted the smiling hostess.

"Hi Jane," Cory returned while he pulled at his wet clothes.

"Here, let me help you with that," Jane offered and helped him slip his jacket off. "Oh my, you're soaked clear through."

"Well, it's really coming down out there," Cory agreed. He looked at his reflection in the glass of the door. He looked a mess. His hair was matted down flat against his head and the shoulders of his green and blue plaid shirt were soaked. Another raindrop found its way down his spine causing him to cringe.

Jane pulled out a dry bar cloth from behind her podium and handed it to him. "Here."

"Thank you," he said. He ran the cloth over his hair and then his shirt, trying to sop up as much of the excess water as he could before handing the cloth back to the hostess. "Is she here?"

"Yes, at your usual table," Jane answered and nodded while she dropped the towel out of sight somewhere beneath her station.

Cory craned his neck to see into the dining room. He spotted Katherine seated with her back toward him. His anxiety level rose. He pressed his eyes closed and took a deep breath.

"Is everything all right?" Jane asked.

Cory opened his eyes and smiled slightly. "Yes, I'm fine. So, how do I look?"

"You look soaked, Mister Martin." Jane answered and gave him an apologetic look.

"It's okay. Thank you for your honesty." Cory smiled.

As he turned to head toward his table, Jane spoke up.

"Oh, happy birthday."

Cory stopped and turned around. His shoulders slumped. "She told you?"

"Yes," Jane grinned.

"I hope she isn't planning anything crazy," he said. "You'd tell me, right?"

"Well—" Jane avoided eye contact.

"Oh dear." Cory glanced at Katherine's back again. He hadn't celebrated his birthday since he was twelve and the thought of it made his anxiety skyrocket inside his chest. "Thank you," he said to Jane and then made his way across the dining room.

The restaurant was surprisingly empty. Unusual for mid-afternoon. *The foul weather was probably the reason.*

Seeing Katherine normally put him at ease. She was the first person he met when he started working at Bank of West in the Financial District. However, today was not normal. He walked up behind her. Her long auburn hair, tied in a ponytail by the cream-colored silk scarf he had given her for her birthday, fell in soft curls down to her shoulders. As he drew nearer he caught the soft scent of her perfume. She was turned slightly, appearing to be looking out at the stormy beach. His stomach tightened and his hands began to tremble. He rubbed them together in an effort to hide it.

"Sorry I'm late," he said and bent down putting his

arms around her, kissing her check.

"Cory! You're soaking wet!" she shrieked and laughed, pulling away from him and wiping her cheek. "Gross!"

He released his hold and slipped into his chair to her right. He quickly took the cloth napkin from the table and opened it over his lap.

"Oh my god," Katherine gasped. She wiped at the dark shadows under Cory's brown eyes as though she could somehow erase them. "You look awful. Haven't you been sleeping?"

"It's been a bit rough," he answered. "You look amazing as always," he said trying to change the subject to her.

Her hand dropped and she sat back in her chair. Her expression changed from concern to confusion and worry.

"What's wrong?" she asked.

Cory shook his head. "It's nothing, really. I just haven't been sleeping very well lately."

"That explains the dark circles but Cory, you look like you've lost more weight."

"Really? I hadn't noticed," he answered and looked down at the front of his shirt. He pulled it away from his stomach in an attempt to look bigger. The truth was, he had noticed and knew why.

"Is this about the book you're writing?" Katherine snapped. "Is that editor of yours giving you grief? Honestly, I don't know why you put up with him."

"No," he shook his head. "Jackson's fine and he's my agent. He's under pressure too from the publishers. But that's not it."

"Then what is it, honey? Tell me. We can face whatever it is together."

Cory looked down at the sparkling diamond engagement ring on Katherine's hand while it rested on his. His stomach tightened more.

The one thing Cory prided himself on was keeping his life in order, scripted like a made-for-TV movie with him directing every detail, every emotion, every camera angle. Now, everything felt as though it were crashing down all around him. He looked into Katherine's eyes. How could he tell her? How could he stop the hurt that was sure to come?

He felt a lump growing in his throat, closing it off. He felt as though he couldn't breathe. His eyes began to tear.

"Kathy, I have to go away."

"Another business trip? That's okay. The wedding isn't for a couple months yet. We have—"

"No," Cory interrupted.

"No?" Katherine cocked her head and eyed him. "What?"

"I am moving back to Oregon."

"But we're getting married."

Cory felt his heart pounding against the inside of his chest like a wild animal wanting to be freed.

"I can't." His voice was near a whisper.

Katherine jerked her hand away. Her look of concern was replaced by one of confusion. She began to fumble with the ring on her finger.

"Wha-what do you mean, I can't? We're getting married."

"I-I," the words were getting stuck in his throat. This was not going the way he had rehearsed it in his mind. "I can't."

"I don't understand." She shook her head. Her eyes teared up and a look of panic came over her.

"Kathy," Cory spoke quietly and reached for her hand. She pulled it away.

"Kathy, you're my best and my dearest friend. I never wanted to hurt you. You have to believe that. I do love you," He looked into her beautiful brown eyes. "But I can't marry you."

The room felt deafeningly quiet. Cory watched Katherine's beautiful face contort as his words entered her ears and slowly registered in her heart. She opened her mouth as if to speak, but nothing came. Tears began to stream down her cheeks but she could not divert her eyes from him.

"I'm sorry," Cory apologized softly.

"B-b-but why?" Katherine choked and cried. Her lips quivered. "What have I done?"

"It's not—"

"Don't! Don't you dare give me that bullshit line," Katherine snapped. She pulled at the ring on her finger but it wouldn't budge. "Damn it!" she cursed.

"But it's true, Kathy," Cory continued. "There are things about me that you don't know. It wouldn't be fair to you."

"What things?" she asked. She wiped the tears from her eyes and glared at him. "What? Tell me! You owe me at least that much."

"I," Cory started to answer while he looked at her. He shook his head. "I'm sorry. I just can't. Not here, not now."

"You bastard!" Katherine slammed her fists down on the table while she jumped up from her chair.

Before Cory could say another word, she rushed out of the restaurant, past a group of waiters headed toward him. The one in the center of the trio held a slice of dark chocolate cake with a scoop of vanilla ice cream on top. He shielded the tiny flame of the candle from the Katherine's wake and gave Cory a confused look.

Cory shook his head.

The waiters dispersed after leaving the plate of dessert on the table.

And they wonder why I never celebrate my birthday.

He blew out the candle.

CHAPTER TWO

The antique mantle clock struck nine. Connie looked at the red brick fireplace from her seat on the couch.

"Where is he?" Pamela huffed and slapped the armrests of her leather, wingback chair.

Connie jumped, nearly spilling her coffee. She looked at her sister-in-law who fidgeted and looked around the living room as though she were about to lose her mind.

"He'll be here," Connie tried to reassure her.

Pamela reached for her water glass that sat on the coffee table between her and her guests but then stood up sharply instead. She ran her hand over the top of her head, through her long, brown hair.

"Honestly," she snapped. "How frigging long does it take?" She walked over to the living room window behind the sofa and pulled back the lace curtain to see the street.

"Pam, don't worry. He'll be here soon," Connie repeated. She turned sideways on the sofa and gave her husband, Mark, a worried glance before looking at Pamela.

"Something's wrong, I just know it," Pamela said shaking her head and running her hand over her very pregnant stomach.

"Why would you think that?" Mark asked.

"He's been gone for almost two hours! He only went to the store for a quart of vanilla ice cream. It's not rocket science." She turned away from the window, wringing her hands and began to pace. "I knew I should've picked it up myself. I knew he'd forget to do it on his way home."

Mark pushed on Connie's leg and then nodded toward Pamela.

"Pamela," she said while she stood up and brushed past Mark. She put her arm around Pamela's shoulders and stopped her from pacing. "Please, try not to worry."

"I wish I could," she scoffed. "Every time he walks out that door to go to work, it's all I seem to do. I knew being a cop's wife was going to be hard but since we found out we are expecting, I can't stop worrying."

"But he's not on duty right now," Mark said.

"Besides, you know how my brother loves to gab. He's probably run into someone he knows and is flapping his jaw," Connie added. "Come, sit back down and try to relax. Worrying isn't good for you or the baby. He'll be back soon. Please, come, sit back down and try to relax."

"I suppose you're right." Pamela walked back over to her chair and sat down. Connie returned to the sofa and took her seat again.

"I just get so frustrated with him sometimes." Pamela said in a defeated tone. "He knows we always get together every year on Cory's birthday and still he manages to be late. I don't know how many times I had remind him of what day it is today and that he needed pick up the ice cream on his way home. I tell you, between this pregnancy and him, I think I'm going to lose my mind."

"Well, you only have three more months to go, then at least one of your problems will be solved," Connie teased.

"True." Pamela grimaced and grabbed her stomach.

Connie sat forward. Her eyebrows pinched in a look of concern. "Pam?"

"It's okay," Pamela said and exhaled. She smiled. "The baby's just throwing a fit, too."

Connie relaxed and sat back on the sofa.

Pamela began to slowly rock her chair. "I know some women love being pregnant, but I have to tell you, I can't wait until this little alien is out."

"Pamela!" Connie gasped.

Mark chuckled out loud.

Pamela laughed. "I'm just teasing…well, sort of. I can't wait to be able to tie my own shoes and fit into my skinny jeans again."

"Well, I hope that works out for you," Connie said.

"What do you mean?" Pamela asked giving her sister-in-law a concerned look.

"It won't happen overnight. It took several months before I lost all the weight I gained when pregnant with Byron; and even then I still wasn't able to wear my old blouses."

"You weren't?" Pamela's mouth dropped open.

"Yeah, 'fraid so. I had to buy all new."

"A bill I gladly paid," Mark chimed in with a grin.

"You men are all alike!" Connie sneered and pushed him away from her. She laughed and looked at her husband, at his blue eyes and square jaw. She felt her pulse quicken and looked away before her mind wandered too far. "But, I'd gladly do it all again."

"You mean you want another one?" Pamela asked.

"If it happened, I wouldn't mind." Connie admitted.

"Oh, not me. When this one is born, that's it for me. No more."

"You say that now, but you'll forget all this stuff."

"Like hell I will. I could live my whole life without throwing up every morning, having puffy ankles and feet to the point I can't wear regular shoes, having all my clothes feel too tight. No, I will never forget."

Connie laughed and took a sip from her coffee cup.

The room fell silent. Connie glanced at Mark who appeared to be inspecting the ceiling and walls around the room.

"Where can he be?" Pamela broke the silence.

Connie looked at her again. "Do you want Mark to go see what's keeping him?"

"Would you?" Pamela asked and looked at him.

Connie turned toward her husband. He was looking at her. She raised her eyebrows in a pleading sort of way.

"Sure," he said. "If it will help."

"Oh that would be great," Pamela answered.

Mark stood up. "I'll grab my—"

"No, don't go," Pamela said stopping him. "If you miss him then we'll be waiting for you. It's okay. Thank you anyway."

Mark looked at Connie who shrugged her shoulders. He bent down and picked up his coffee mug.

"Anyone want more coffee?"

"Sure," Connie answered and handed him her cup.

"None for me," Pamela said. "The doc has taken me off caffeine. Won't even let me have decaf. Said I would be too tempted to drink the hard stuff. So, it's just water and juices."

"Can I get you some more water then?" Mark offered.

"No, I'm fine. Thank you."

Connie watched Mark disappear into the kitchen. She looked around the room. "I really love these old Portland Craftsman houses. They feel so warm and homey."

"Yeah, that was one thing Kyle and I agreed on right away. He said it reminds him of the house you grew up in and I couldn't argue with that. They do feel nice."

Mark walked back into the living room and carefully handed Connie her cup of coffee. He took a sip from his while he sat back down beside her.

"Have you and Kyle decided when you're going to tell his dad about this?"

"Mark!" Connie gasped.

Mark looked at his wife and shrugged his shoulders while mouthing the word, what?

"It's okay, Connie. Kyle and I have discussed it and he doesn't ever want to tell Jack about the baby. With the way Jack drinks and how he's treated all of us and especially Cory over the years, the baby doesn't need to be subjected to that."

"But Pam, Dad and Stella only live across town. Forest Grove isn't that big. People will talk. He's bound to find out sooner or later." Connie protested.

"That's true," Mark concurred. "It's not like we live in Portland. Stella has her spies. Trust me, he *will* find out."

"I know," Pamela said and nodded.

She appeared nervous again but in a different way. Connie set her cup down on the coffee table.

"That's why Kyle's applied for a job with the Seattle P.D."

"No!" Connie gasped. She felt her eyes begin to tear. "You can't move and leave me here alone." She grabbed Mark's hand and squeezed it tight.

"It's not definite. They haven't answered or offered him a job yet."

"But if they do, then you'll be moving away." Connie felt her chest and throat tighten. She knew that tears were next.

"It's going to be okay," Mark tried to reassure her while the pried her ever tightening fingers from his hand.

"You say that but if they move it won't be," she said. Tears began to find their way down her cheeks. "First Cory leaves and now you three. I don't think I can take it." She felt Mark's arm around her shoulders while he pulled her closer.

"We will be okay. Seattle isn't that far. We can visit often."

"Connie, it's not definite," Pamela said.

"I know," Connie answered and dried her cheeks on the handkerchief Mark gave her. "It's just you and Kyle are all the family I have close by."

"Changing the subject," Mark said while he continued to cradle Connie under his arm. "Have you two decided on any names for the baby?"

Pamela stopped rocking for a moment, putting one hand on her round stomach. "I'd like to name the baby after Kyle if it's a boy, but Kyle wants to name him Graham after my father."

"Oh no!" Connie gasped shaking her head. She sat up, suddenly composed. "You can't let him do that. You know how utterly horrible kids can be. They would tease him mercilessly. 'Graham cracker, Graham cracker,'" she chanted in a high pitched, childlike voice.

"Yes," Pamela laughed and nodded. "I know."

"Well, I'm with you. Kyle Junior would be a much better name."

"That is if it's a boy," Pamela interrupted. "If it's a girl, we are naming her after your mother and mine, Emily Rose."

Connie smiled.

"Wait a minute," Mark spoke up. "You mean to tell us you and Kyle don't know what you're having?" He gave her a curious look.

"I know it seems old fashioned, but there are too few real surprises in life anymore. We told the doctors we don't want to know," Pamela explained.

"I don't care either way," Connie said, smiling once again. "Boy or girl, I'm going to be an aunt! Aunt Connie," she said proudly.

Just then, the sound of a car pulling into the driveway

broke into the conversation. Pamela jumped in surprise.

"Well, it's about time!" she said indignantly.

"See, we told you he'd be home soon." Mark said as he looked over his shoulder at the window.

"I'll go warm up the pie," Pamela said and quickly disappeared into the kitchen.

"Boy is Kyle gonna catch it when he walks in," Connie whispered to Mark.

"Just remember," he said quietly taking her hand and giving it a firm squeeze. "Stay out of it. It's between them."

"Oh, I will," Connie reassured him, pulling her hand free. "Believe me. Getting in the middle of Kyle's problems is the last thing I want to do."

The front doorbell chimed.

"Connie," Pamela called from the kitchen. "Will you get that? He's probably forgotten his key."

"Okay," Connie answered back with a confused look. She glanced at Mark and stood up. "How could he forget his key when it's on the same key ring as his car keys?" she whispered.

"Maybe his hands are full," Mark suggested but rose to his feet.

"How full could they be, he only went for ice cream?" She said over her shoulder.

The doorbell chimed again.

"I'm coming," Connie called and reached for the doorknob and gave it a turn. "Boy, are you in-" Connie froze as she stood in the open doorway. "Oh, Tom," she gave a little nervous chuckle. "I thought you were Kyle. He isn't here right now. He went out to get some ice cream. He should be back any minute. Would you like to come in and wait for him?" She began to talk faster and faster when she noticed the somber expression on Tom's face. "He shouldn't be much longer, really. He's been gone for a couple hours and you know how he loves to talk to people. We're sure he must have run into someone he knows. He should be back any minute." Her voice was becoming shrill and she started to repeat herself. "He shouldn't be much longer, really. Really!" she yelled and began to tremble, tears filling her eyes.

Mark rushed to Connie's side and put his arm around her to steady her trembling body. He glanced up at the young, dark haired officer, Kyle's partner. "Please, won't you come in?" he invited, gently moving Connie away from the door.

Tom took a step into the foyer. He fumbled nervously with his cap. Another officer, much older and balding, stepped into the foyer beside him. Mark recognized the man as Kyle's captain on the force.

"Mark, Connie," Tom said, his voice cracking like a pubescent teen. "I need to speak to Pamela. Is she home?"

"Well, it's about time," Pamela said as she bounced into the dining room with the steaming, hot peach pie in her mitted hands. Her smile faded instantly and the color drained from her cheeks when her eyes met Tom's. Her entire body began to tremble.

"No!" she screamed.

The glass pie-plate slipped from her hands and shattered at her feet.

CHAPTER THREE

The scent of freshly brewed coffee filled the kitchen while Cory poured himself a cup. He walked over to the refrigerator and opened it. The shelves were bare except for a solitary carton of non-dairy creamer. It was not as good as the real thing, but since he'd become lactose intolerant, he'd grown used to it. He closed the refrigerator door and added the creamer to his coffee.

Taking a sip, he looked around the empty kitchen. Everything he owned was safely packed in cardboard boxes, ready for the movers who were due at any minute. He walked through the swinging door into the dining room.

The dining room echoed, empty except for an antique table and six chairs that were wrapped in heavy, quilted moving blankets and bound by plastic wrap.

He walked into the living room, looked around. Boxes, taped shut and labeled, lined the far wall in the entry hall and overflowed into the living room. Even the old grandfather clock, with its weights and pendulum safely removed and secured, stood wrapped in a padded moving blanket, ready for the movers. Cory made his way around the stacks of boxes to the dark, brown velvet sofa. He set his coffee mug down on top of a box labeled "kitchen" and then sat down at the end of the sofa.

He was still amazed at the amount of stuff he had accumulated over the last ten years. When he moved into his condo, he had only a bed and could count the number of boxes on one hand. Now he needed several hands.

He picked up his messenger bag that was tucked between the arm of the sofa and a short stack of boxes. He hesitated for a moment before he opened it. Two envelopes lay on top of his laptop computer. He took them out and closed the flap. With a deep breath, he opened the first envelope. Saint Mary's Medical Center was printed in bold type across the letterhead. Beneath it was Dignity Health Cardiac Care.

He quickly scanned the page. He didn't need to read it; he had already memorized it. He stuffed the letter back into its envelope then tucked it away in the pocket of his sport coat. He draped the coat carefully over the back of the sofa.

He stared at the other envelope marked Alaska Airlines. By this time tomorrow he'd be back in Oregon, miles away from the life he'd made for himself in San Francisco. He shook his head, smiling in disbelief.

"What life?" he said to the room. "It was nothing but a bunch of well-scripted lies. Written down and studied until I knew them by heart. Hell, I've repeated so many times, I even began to believe them myself."

They were lies about being an only child and raised by a loving parents who encouraged him to follow his dreams. Their home was filled with love and joy. When it came time for him to move out, it was hard but he knew he had to follow his heart.

Hearing them in his head, all that was missing was the white picket fence.

"I can't believe anyone actually bought that crap," he said and shook his head. Disgusted with himself more than anyone.

But they weren't complete lies, a voice in his head whispered. *There was a point when it was true, before you twelfth birthday, before the nightmare began.*

He placed the ticket back into its envelope and leaned against the back of the sofa. He rubbed his face and eyes with his hands, tipping his head back and staring at the ceiling. He brought his head forward until his eyes came to rest on the empty wall above the gas fireplace.

"Oh, Mama," he sighed out loud. "Why did you do it? Why?"

Suddenly, a flash, a memory.

The warm, October sun shone down on Cory while he hurried home from school with his friends, Paul and Todd. The three had been together since kindergarten, inseparable like the three musketeers. In fact, that was their favorite after school game, sword fighting with long sticks in the backyard for hours.

"What time is your party?" asked Paul, the tallest and oldest of the three. He gave Cory a playful nudge. "Curb you dog," he laughed when Cory stepped off the sidewalk into the street to keep from falling over.

"Quimby!" Cory retorted, jumping back onto the sidewalk. If they weren't such good friends, Cory was sure he wouldn't like Paul. Paul was too much of a bully. "My mom said after school. So, I guess tomorrow around four would be okay," Cory answered and shrugged.

"That's cool," nodded Todd. Todd was the shortest boy in class. His blonde hair, his blue eyes and his freckled nose endeared him to all the girls in the seventh grade. "I think I can skip soccer practice for one afternoon. Coach won't be too mad."

"What do you mean?" Paul laughed, tossing his binder into the air and catching it. "He probably won't even miss you. He never lets you play anyway."

"I don't care," answered Todd. He shrugged indifferently. "My dad's the one who wants me to play."

"Speaking of dads, my dad said he saw your dad coming out of Shuck's Tavern last night," Paul said to Cory in a tone that sounded shocked and superior.

"I know." Cory shrugged and looked at the sidewalk under his feet while he walked. Ever since his mother's diagnoses of cancer, his father had taken to drinking. The worse she became, the more his father drank. Lately, he seemed to be drunk all of the time.

"I can't believe I'm finally going to be twelve years old tomorrow." Cory said changing the subject.

"Ah, you're still the youngest kid in the class," Todd teased in a baby voice. "Such a widdo baby," he mocked and tried to pinch Cory's cheek, but Cory pulled away just in time.

"I am not a baby!" Cory protested, glaring at Todd.

"Cory Martin!" a gruff masculine voice shouted from across the lawn. "Get in here at once! You boys, go on home!"

"Hi, Mister Martin. Bye, Mister Martin," Todd and Paul greeted with a wave and forced smile. "See you in school tomorrow, Cory."

"See ya' guys tomorrow," Cory called and nodded as his friends continued on their way.

"It's about time you got home. Your sister and brother have been home for almost a half an hour. Where've you been?"

"Nowhere, honest. I came straight home."

Smack! A sharp pain and then a burning sensation on the back of his head. Cory fought back the tears that immediately filled his eyes. If there was one thing his father hated, it was a boy who cried. "Take it like a man," his father would say.

"Don't you dare cry, boy!" Jack ordered. He took another drink of his beer. "Get your books put away and then your mother wants to see you. Why, I'll never know. Hurry up, boy!"

Cory quickly rushed up the stairs to his bedroom and hung his jacket and backpack on the wall hooks right inside his door. He quietly walked across the hall and knocked lightly on his mother's door. He didn't wait for an answer but slowly opened the door and stuck his head inside.

The heavy drapes on the window across the room were pulled shut blocking all but a sliver of light. Framed photographs of the family taken through the years covered the dresser against the wall to his left. Wilted red roses drooped in a crystal vase behind them. Cory stepped quietly inside the room.

The sterile scent of Lysol did little to mask the smell of sickness. A single hospital bed with its head set against the wall sat right in front of the door. It replaced the queen-sized bed his parents shared. The head of the bed was kept slightly raised so his mother could see the pictures upon waking. Beside the bed stood a tall tray table, another hospital equipment rental. A tissue box, empty glass with a straw and pitcher of iced water were the only items on the tray table. Cory walked over to the chair beside the bed.

He looked at the frail figure of a woman whose form he could barely see beneath the blankets. Her thin hands, bruised and blackened by the spreading cancer, were folded over her stomach on top of the blankets. Her face looked like that of an elderly woman, not one of a thirty-three year old. Her once long, thick auburn hair was gone, replaced by short, white stubble, the result of months of chemotherapy.

"Mama?" Cory whispered.

Slowly Emily Martin opened her eyes. She slowly turned her head to look at Cory, furrowing her eyebrows as though even the slightest movement caused her great pain. Slowly her expression softened and her lips curled up in a loving smile.

"Ah, you're home," she breathed in a murmur.

"Yes, Mama, I'm home." Cory repeated and stepped up next to the bed.

"Come. Sit down. There's something I need to tell you,

dear." She licked her pale, chapped lips. Cory sat down on the edge of the chair beside the bed. "It's very important. I want you to know this before-" she paused to catch her breath.

Cory felt a wave of panic. "You aren't going to die, Mama. You promised, 'not in a million years.' Remember? You promised."

"Cory. Cory," Emily raised a weak hand to hush him. "No more. We both know the truth. I'm dying, son."

"No," Cory whimpered, tears beginning to stream down his cheeks.

"Yes, son. Listen to me, now. I have something to tell you. You have to listen."

Cory dried his tears and struggled to compose himself. "I-I'm listening, Mama."

"Cory, I'm leaving this house to you. When I'm gone, the it's yours. It belonged to your father's parents and I want you and your sister and brother to live here."

"But-" Cory started to protest, confused. Again, Emily put her hand up.

"Cory, Jack is not your real father."

The words hit Cory like an exploding bomb in his ears, sending him sinking back into the chair. His thoughts reeled with a flood with questions.

"I-I don't understand, Mama."

"Your real father was John Walker. He was killed in a car accident when you were almost two years old and I was pregnant with your sister," Emily continued. "Jack was a dear friend and took care of us and helped me get through the loss of your father. He's a good man, Cory. I know he's a bit rough at times, but he really does love you and your sister as though you were his own. You mustn't tell Connie. She's too young to understand right now. When I'm gone, I want you to promise me you'll take care of the family. Be strong for me. Be strong for them. Can you do that?"

"Y-y-yes, Mama," Cory nodded, wasn't sure what she wanted him to do. He felt numb from the news. The man he had known as his father wasn't really his dad?

"Cory, I have something special for you. For your birthday." She smiled but it vanished quickly. Cory knew she was growing tired. "It's in the top drawer of my dresser." She tried to raise her hand to point across the room but it barely rose off the blanket. "Go open it."

Cory rose to his feet and approached the dresser as though he were afraid of it. Ever since he could remember, the dresser, even this bedroom was off limits to him and his sister and brother. They were never to go in either. Carefully he opened the top drawer.

"It's in the small white box just under the handkerchiefs."

Cory moved the handkerchiefs and took out the small, thin, white box. Before he closed the drawer, he made careful attention to put the handkerchiefs back neatly. He returned to his chair with the box.

"Now don't open it until tomorrow," Emily instructed with a smile, playfully.

"I won't, Mama." Cory nodded and looked at the box.

"It was your father's," Emily said and became still.

"My father's?" Cory said looking at the box and then at his mother. "Mama?" Slowly he rose to his feet while a feeling of panic rose inside him. He watched her chest rise and fall and felt his fears ebb away. He leaned over and kissed her cheek.

"I love you, Mama," he whispered.

He quietly backed into the hall and closed the bedroom door. Staring at the box in his hand and trying to make sense of what his mother said, he turned around and bumped into Jack. He jumped back and nearly let out a scream but stifled it quickly.

"Sorry," he said not knowing if he was supposed to still call him Dad or not.

"So, what's in the box?" Jack asked.

"I-I don't know. Mama said not to open it until tomorrow."

"You took that out of her drawer, didn't you?" Jack said gruffly.

"Yes," Cory admitted. "But—"

"Hand it over, right now!"

"It's my birthday present," Cory explained.

Before the words had finished leaving Cory's lips, Jack slapped the side of Cory's head sharply. Cory stumbled and fell against the wall. He held up the box.

"Don't sass me boy! I'll mop the floor with you," he snapped and snatched the box.

Cory opened his mouth to speak but the words wouldn't come. He put his hand quickly to his burning cheek as tears fell from his brown eyes.

"Not another word! Now go get dinner ready," Jack ordered.

"Yes, sir."

"That's right. It's *Sir*. And don't you ever forget it."

The next day, Cory sat staring out the window of his classroom, daydreaming. He couldn't wait until the final bell rang and school was over for the day. The moment it sounded, he jumped to his feet and rushed out the door. He had just enough time to get home and get things ready for his birthday party. He was still slipping his backpack on when he started across the parking lot toward the sidewalk.

"Cory," a woman called to him.

Cory recognized the voice of his Aunt Agnes, his mother's sister, immediately. He stopped and turned around. He had walked past her classic brown 1964 Mustang without seeing it.

"Auntie Ag?" he said while he walked back to her.

She stood up from leaning against her car and put her cigarette out on the blacktop. Cory felt his cheeks blush when he noticed the nipples of her large breasts beneath her tight tank top. She always wore tight clothes that made him feel uncomfortable.

"Auntie Ag, what are you doing here?" he asked when he walked up to her.

"Well, I-I- Where are your sister and brother?"

"They should be out any minute. I have to get home and get things ready for my party. See you later, okay?"

"No," Agnes called and raised a halting hand. "Cory, wait. Your father sent me to pick the three of you up."

Cory turned and faced his aunt. "Why? What's wrong?" Then, he saw her eyes. They were red and wet with tears.

"No!" Cory screamed. "She can't. It's my birthday! She

can't!" Without warning, he turned around and took off running for home.

"Cory! Please wait!" Agnes called after him.

Cory didn't stop. He ran as fast as he could. His heart pounded in his chest until it hurt. When he reached his block, he stopped. Parked in front of his house were a police car and a black hearse.

"No!" he groaned and rushed across the lawn.

The front door opened and a man dressed in a white hospital-like uniform stepped outside. He turned back to the doorway and lifted the end of a gurney across the threshold and set it down on the porch. Cory felt a glimmer of relief when he saw the large black bag that covered the top of the bed. He watched the two men lower the gurney down the steps onto the front walk. While the men wheeled it past him, Cory noticed something was in the zippered bag. His chest tightened. His mind went blank.

"No," he screamed.

The two men stopped and looked at Cory. They looked at each other.

"I'm sorry, son," the man nearest Cory said. His expression was compassionate.

The lead man motioned with his head for them to keep moving. They wheeled the gurney over to the hearse.

"Mama!" Cory screamed, tears streaming down his face, his hands reaching out for her. He started toward them.

"Cory! Get back here!" Jack's voice thundered angrily. "Get in the house!"

Cory halted in his tracks. He looked at Jack then back

at the men loading the gurney into the hearse.

"Now!" Jack yelled.

The door of the hearse slammed shut.

Cory spun around and rushed into the house, running to his mother's bedroom. He threw open the door and looked into the room. Sunlight poured in through the window. The thick drapes were gone. The hospital bed was stripped of its sheets and bedding. The dresser was cleared of the photographs and wilted flowers. The bedroom looked sterile with no evidence his mother had ever been there.

"She's gone, Cory," Agnes said from behind him.

Cory didn't move. He stood frozen in place, staring blindly at the cold, lifeless room. His mind seemed caught in a whirlwind. He heard noises, voices around him, but he didn't understand them.

This can't be happening, not now, not today.

It is happening. She's dead. There's going to be a funeral, cards and flowers.

No! It's my birthday. I'm supposed to have a party, my friends, a cake, and presents.

She's dead.

"No! No!" He pressed his hands over his ears in an attempt to block the voices he heard arguing back and forth.

This is a bad dream, a nightmare. Any minute now I'll wake up. That's it. It's not real. It's not happening.

It is real. She's gone. She's not coming back.

"But I'm not ready, Mama. I don't know what you want me to do. Help me, Mama," Cory cried out and fell to his knees on the bedroom floor. Tears blurred his vision.

"Cory, dear," Agnes said and took him by his shoulders. She pulled him to his feet. "She's gone, honey. She's no longer in any pain."

"But…" Cory continued to weep.

"Come on, it's time for dinner." Agnes turned him around toward the hallway.

Cory looked at the doorway and saw Connie peeking into the room. Her cheeks were damp from tears.

"Cory?" she said in a frightened tone.

Suddenly his strength returned. He walked away from his aunt's grasp and went to his sister. He put his arms around her and hugged her. "It's going to be okay," he whispered into her ear. "Come on."

The three made their way down the hall and down the stairs to the dining room.

"Well, look who decided to join us," Jack slurred as Cory and Connie took their seat at the table. "Get me another beer!" he ordered.

"Jack," Agnes said gently, "Don't you think you've had enough for now? You don't need another—"

"Don't you tell me what I need!" Jack yelled, hammering his fist down hard on the tabletop and causing the glasses and dishes to jump. "This is my house, goddamnit!" he glared directly at Cory.

Agnes jumped and took a step back.

Cory stood up to go for the beer.

"No, sit down, Cory, I'll get it," Agnes said while she stomped to the kitchen. Cory heard the refrigerator door open and the bottle on the shelves rattle. The was the unmistakable sound of a bottle being opened and then Agnes marched back into the room. She slammed the bottle down in front of Jack.

"Here!" she snapped at him. "What my sister ever saw in you is beyond me. I hope you choke on it," she muttered under her breath but Cory heard her. She turned to look at her young niece and nephews and her expression softened. "Try to eat something. I have a special cake for dessert."

"There'll be no dessert tonight!" Jack shouted. His eyes were red and bloodshot. His cheeks were damp.

"But it's Cory's—"

Jack jumped to his feet and grabbed the edge of the table to keep from falling down. "I said no dessert!" he shouted. "Now eat your dinner and go to bed, all of you!" He turned and staggered into the living room.

"We can still have your cake," Agnes whispered and stroked Cory's hair.

"That's okay, Auntie Ag. I'm not really hungry."

"Then we'll save it for tomorrow."

The next morning, Cory awoke to the smell of bacon and hot coffee. He looked at the small clock on his nightstand and jumped out of bed when he saw it was nearly eight-thirty. He quickly changed into his school clothes, made his bed before hurrying downstairs.

Connie and Kyle were seated at the dining room table still in their pajamas. Jack sat with his elbows on the table and holding a cup of black coffee above his plate of eggs, bacon and pancakes.

"Sorry I'm late," Cory said and slipped into his chair.

Jack didn't respond.

Cory looked at his siblings. "Why aren't you dressed for school?"

"Dad said we don't have to go today," Connie spoke up.

"We don't have to go until after the funeral," Kyle added.

"We don't?" Cory looked at Jack.

Jack shook his head.

"Here you go," Agnes said while she sat a plate of steaming hot pancakes in front of Cory. "There are bacon and eggs if you want some." She motioned at the platters in the center of the table.

"Thank you," Cory said. He reached for the butter dish. The delicious aromas had awakened his stomach and appetite.

"Hey, Cory," Kyle spoke up. "Look what Dad gave me."

Cory looked across the table at his eight-year-old brother. His eyes widened and his mouth dropped open when he saw the thin white box his mother had given him. He glanced at Jack who lowered his coffee cup slightly and gave him a smug look back.

Cory looked back at Kyle in time to see him pull a gold pocket watch from the box.

"It's a little clock on a chain," Kyle announced.

"It's a pocket watch," Jack corrected. He set his coffee down and took the watch from Kyle. "Train conductors used to wear them back in the olden days. They wore vests with a tiny pocket just big enough for their watch. It was their job to keep the train on schedule."

"Cool," Kyle said and looked at the watch again.

"But that was my—" Cory stopped himself when Jack looked at him.

"What was that?" Jack asked.

Cory looked at Connie who was busy eating her breakfast, seemingly ignoring Kyle and the watch.

"Nothing," Cory answered.

"No, you were about to say something. I'd like to hear it." Jack goaded.

"It's okay," Cory said. He looked at his younger brother who was still playing with the watch. "It's a nice present, Kyle."

Kyle looked up and smiled.

"Eat you breakfast." Jack said in a stern tone.

Cory returned to buttering the pancakes on his plate but his appetite had vanished. Instead his stomach tightened in a big knot. He put his knife down.

"I guess I'm not hungry after all," he said.

"Fine, then you can start clearing the table," Jack said. He picked up his plate and dropped it on top of Cory's. "Give your aunt a hand in the kitchen while you're at it." Jack took another sip of his coffee.

"Yes, sir." Cory answered.

He stood and began to clear away his dishes. Agnes moved aside letting Cory slip by her into the kitchen.

"What was all of that about?" she asked and followed him over to the sink.

"Nothing." Cory answered.

"Come on," Agnes insisted.

"Mom gave me that box and told me not to open it

until my birthday. She said it belonged to my real dad."

"How did Jack get it?"

"He took it from me."

Agnes looked over her shoulder in the direction of the dining room. "That dirty s.o.b."

"It's okay, let Kyle keep it."

"No, it is yours."

"Please," Cory pleaded and watched his aunt walk into the dining room.

"Jack," she spoke up sharply, folding her arms over her chest. "That was uncalled for."

"What was uncalled for?" Jack asked.

"Oh knock it off! You know damned well that watch was meant for Cory."

"I know no such thing! And the last time I looked, the name on the mailbox is mine," Jack barked back and rose to his feet. "So, I suggest you do us all a favor and leave."

"Well!" Agnes said in a huff. "I will not stand here and be treated like I'm some sort of stranger. I'm part of this family."

"There's the door!" Jack yelled back and pointed in the direction of the front door. "Oh, and another thing," he continued. "Since Emily's gone, we're no longer family and you're not welcome in this house. You can pass that on to the rest of your crack pot family."

Agnes turned and looked at Kyle, Connie and Cory, who had just returned to the dining room. She frowned looking at them.

"If you ever need anything," she spoke directly to them. "You have my phone number."

"They won't be needing it!" Jack rushed at Agnes, grabbing her arm. "Now get out of this house!" He pulled her toward the front door, opened it and pushed her out, slamming the door behind her.

"What're you standing there for?" Jack yelled looking directly at Cory. "Get back in that kitchen and get it cleaned!" he ordered.

Cory grabbed a plater from the table and returned to the kitchen.

"Dad?" Cory hear Kyle's voice.

"Put the watch back in your pocket. I gave it to you. It's yours. Don't listen to a word that woman says."

The front doorbell rang, jolting Cory back to the present and nearly spilling his coffee on himself. He looked at his wristwatch.

"They can't be here already," he said and looked around at the stacks of boxes that filled his living room. The doorbell rang again. "Coming!" he shouted and jumped up.

He opened the front door.

"Kathy!" he gasped, happy to see her and yet nervous at the same time. He started to give her their usual embrace but she stepped back, a reminder that things had changed between them. He glanced at her hand. The ring was gone.

"May I come in?"

"Of course," he said and stepped aside. He held the door open for her. "Please excuse the mess."

Katherine walked into the foyer and froze. She let out a gasp and covered her mouth with her hand.

"What?" Cory asked while he closed the door.

"Nothing," she replied and continued toward the living room.

"Would you like a cup of coffee?"

"Coffee would be fine," she answered in a tone that was anything but fine.

Cory rushed passed her and into the kitchen. While he poured coffee into a disposable cup, he felt anxiety fill his insides. The last thing he wanted was another confrontation with her before he flew back to Oregon.

When he returned to the living room, Katherine was standing by the couch with her back toward him. She appeared to be looking at the sofa. Cory's eyes widened when he saw his plane ticket on the center cushion.

"Here you go," he said nervously and handed her the cup. "Sorry about the paper cup, all of my dishes…are…packed." His voice trailed off. He quickly scooped up his ticket and tucked it into his back pocket. "Care to sit down?"

Katherine tucked one leg under her and sat down at the opposite end of the sofa from Cory. She turned to face him. He could see that her eyes were still red and she looked tired.

He opened his mouth to speak but she beat him to it.

"I wanted to come by. I didn't like the way we left things last night," she said.

"I understand," Cory said with a nod.

Katherine held her hand up to silence him.

"This is hard enough. Let me speak. Cory, I don't understand. Why?"

"Why?"

"I know you don't want to marry me but why do you have to move?"

Cory sat mirroring Katherine. He rubbed his forehead and tried to collect his thoughts.

"There are things about me that you don't know."

"If you say that one more time, I swear I will slap you!" Katherine seethed. "What things? Talk to me, Cory. Tell me. Help me understand. You owe me that much."

Cory looked away. How could he tell his best friend that everything he had told her was a lie? He'd made up a fictional past and, like one of his many novels, it wasn't real. He didn't have a happy childhood. His parents weren't society folks. He'd never even been to the opera or the symphony until they went together last year. Moreover, before her, he had never even had a girlfriend, much less kissed a girl. He looked back at Katherine.

"I don't know where to begin," he answered and looked at the boxes while he tried to collect his thoughts and put them in an order that would make sense.

"Have you ever wished you were someone else?" he asked. "Not anyone special like a movie star or famous person, just anyone but you?"

Katherine stared at him intently, not responding to him, but obviously listening to his every word.

Nervously, Cory began to unravel the lies.

"The day she died, on my twelfth birthday, everything changed. I no longer knew who I was or where I belonged. I guess you could say, I became like those people in that movie; you know, like the living dead. Someone who moves from one day to the next without really living, laughing, or feeling.

"I never celebrated my birthday again," Cory explained. "Instead, my sister—"

"You have a sister?" Katherine gasped.

"Yes, Connie. She's two years younger than me. She's married and has a son. I also have a younger brother, Kyle. He's a policeman back home. He's married and they are expecting their first child."

"Why didn't you tell me about them?"

"I don't know," Cory answered. "I guess, in a way, by not telling you about them I didn't have to feel responsible for them anymore."

"That's crazy," Katherine said, apparently still holding onto her anger at him.

Cory shrugged it off and continued.

"Life after our mother died was much different. I'd get up every morning before the rest of the family. I'd make my bed, shower and dress for school. Then I'd go downstairs and start making breakfast for everyone. Once the coffee finished brewing I'd pour Sir, that's what my step-father told me to call him, a cup and take it upstairs to him. On my way back down to the kitchen I'd wake up Connie and Kyle.

"Sir insisted on having a big breakfast which meant a bowl of hot oatmeal sprinkled with Total cereal, a plate of scrambled eggs, a pancake or two slices of toast and orange juice. So, while they all ate, I'd make and pack their lunches for the day. You know, I don't remember ever eating breakfast. There just wasn't time." Cory paused, staring at the floor, fighting the familiar feelings that began to stir deep inside him. He took a deep breath and let it out slowly.

"After everyone finished their breakfast, I'd quickly clear the table and wash the dishes. Then it was back to my bedroom to await inspection.

"Sir insisted on a spotless bedroom. If anything were left on the floor, he would take it and throw it out, regardless of whether it was a schoolbook, homework, a winter coat or toy. If he found it on the floor, it was in the garbage can and heaven help the person who tried to get it back.

"He was also very particular about how the beds were made. He carried a special coin and if he couldn't bounce that coin off the made bed, it wasn't made properly. For punishment he'd strip off all of the bedding and the offender would sleep a week without sheets, pillowcase, or blankets. There were times I was sure he purposely caused the coin not to bounce. Come winter, like clockwork, I knew I'd be sleeping without bedding."

"That's horrible!" Katherine gasped. Her tone had softened.

Cory glanced at her and then back at the floor.

"The rules didn't apply to everyone to the same degree," he continued. "Sir was extremely strict when it came to my bedroom, but he was a bit more lenient with Connie. I figured it was because she didn't know the truth about him, that he was her step-father and not her real dad. I wish I didn't know. Oh, but Kyle was the only person who could do no wrong, or at least, who didn't have to personally suffer the consequences.

"I don't remember just when it started but Sir made it my responsibility to make sure Kyle's bedroom was clean and ready for inspection. At first, I didn't give it much thought since Kyle was four years younger and still a little kid. But then, Sir decided to take it further. If Kyle's room didn't pass inspection, it was I, not Kyle, who suffered the consequences. I remember thinking that when Kyle reached his tenth birthday the situation would change. But two years later, nothing had except Sir became more volatile."

The morning sun shone through Cory's bedroom window, waking him from his sleep. He looked at the clock on his nightstand.

"Oh my god!" he gasped and jumped out of bed. He rushed into the hall to check the time on the grandfather's clock. It was true. He had overslept by an hour. He quickly made his bed and dressed for school. Rushing downstairs to make breakfast for everyone.

After cleaning the breakfast dishes, Cory ran up the stairs to his bedroom for inspection. Jack was already standing in the doorway. Cory followed him into the bedroom.

"What's this?" Jack asked after picking three sheets of paper off the floor.

Cory looked at his desk. His term paper was gone. He was confused. He was sure they were on his desk when he went downstairs. He looked back at his step-father.

"It's my term paper," Cory admitted. "I don't know how it ended up on the floor."

"You know the rules—"

"Please, don't throw it away. I have to turn it in today."

"If it was that important, why was it on the floor?"

"I don't know. I left it on my desk when I went to bed last night. I-It must have fallen off when I made my bed?"

Jack looked at the papers and his stern expression softened. He started to hand the papers to Cory.

"Not fair!" Kyle shouted from the doorway.

Cory turned sharply and glared at his brother. "Kyle, keep out of this," he snapped.

When Cory turned back to Jack, Jack had taken back his hand and instead held the assignment in both hands.

"Sir?" Cory said.

Jack's jaw tightened. "Rules are rules," he said and then came the awful sound of three hours' work being reduced to small scraps of paper.

"Don't you ever that again!" Jack said and continued to inspect the room.

Cory glanced at the door. Kyle stood with his arms folded over his chest and a smug grin on his face.

"You call this bed made?" Jack asked.

Cory turned around and looked at his bed. He watched while Jack tried to bounce his coin off it but the coin fell flat. A sinking feeling came over Cory.

"Didn't you make your bed this morning?" Jack asked.

"Yes, sir. Right after I got up."

"Well, it doesn't look like it. The corners are untucked, the bedspread is wrinkled, this isn't how we make a bed."

Cory didn't move. Instead, he watched while Jack

ripped the bedding from the bed and bundled it up.

"This is the second week in a row, Cory," Jack said. "When are you going to learn?"

"But—"

"No excuses!" Jack picked up the bundle and left the room.

Slowly Cory dropped down onto his bed. He looked at his brother still standing in the hall outside his bedroom.

"Why Kyle? What did I ever do to you?" he asked.

"I was only playing," Kyle answered.

"Well, thanks a lot. Go away."

Kyle hesitated. His smug expression turned to regret. "I'm sorry."

Cory stood up and closed the door.

That night, after everyone had gone to bed, Cory changed into his pajamas. He took his coat and terrycloth bathrobe from his closet. He looked at his bed and realized his pillow was gone. He looked under his bed and in his closet before he realized that Jack must have taken it with the rest of the sheets and bedspread.

Cory curled up in the corner of his bed and covered himself with his robe. He used his coat as a pillow. Part of him hated Jack and wanted nothing to do with him; yet at the same time, another part of him longed to have the same love and attention Jack showered on Kyle or even Connie.

"Why, Mama, why did you have to tell me?" Cory croaked; weeping until, finally exhausted, he fell asleep.

Summer was a welcome change. It meant that Cory wouldn't have to rush so much in the mornings. Since he wouldn't have to make lunches for school, he had a few extra minutes each morning to make sure his and Kyle's bedrooms passed inspection. Then while Jack was at work, he was free to do his other chores.

One afternoon, while walking home from the grocery store with Connie, Cory noticed a beat up, old, blue Honda Civic drive by.

"A garbage can on wheels," he said and laughed. Connie laughed too. They watched the car turn around and headed back toward them. Suddenly, Cory felt panicked.

"Do you think he heard me?"

"How could he? That thing was making too much noise."

The car pulled up next to the curb and stopped in front of Cory and Connie. They watched the man in the driver's seat lean over toward the passenger window.

"Hey, you're a Martin kid aren't you?" he asked Cory, ignoring Connie.

Cory looked at the man and made a mental note: short, crew cut, black hair; beady eyes; sort of resembles a turtle. "Yes, sir."

"I know your dad, Jack," he smirked.

Yellow teeth, big nose, Cory added another note.

"Say, how would you like to earn some extra money for Christmas?"

"Sure," Cory grinned at the thought. "How?"

"Delivering The Journal newspaper every afternoon."

"Oh," the smile faded from Cory's lips. "I'll have to ask my—" The word stuck in his throat. "I'll have to ask permission first," he answered.

"I understand," the man nodded and began to dig in

his breast pocket. He pulled out a small white piece of paper and handed it to Cory. "Here's my name and phone number, call me if you decide you want to make some money."

Cory looked at the card and watched the funny looking man drive off.

"Do you think dad will let you have a job?" Connie asked.

"I don't know. I doubt it." Cory answered. Still while they walked the rest of the way home, Cory let his mind wander. He thought about what would he buy Connie and Kyle for Christmas if he had the money. Connie wanted a banjo. He wondered how much they cost. Kyle asked for a racetrack for the last three Christmases, maybe…

"You should ask him anyway," Connie said. "Maybe he'll surprise you."

Cory smiled at his sister. "We'll see."

Jack seemed in an good mood when he sat down to dinner. He was actually smiling for the first time since— well a long time.

"Dinner looks good for a change," he said when Cory set the meatloaf platter down.

Cory smiled but didn't say anything. He finished bringing out the potatoes, gravy, green beans, and rolls before sitting down.

Everyone seemed in a good mood, Cory thought while he listened to them talking and laughing. *Maybe I could ask him after dinner?* Cory looked at the card again.

"Hey, dad," Connie said. "Me and Cory met a friend of yours on the way home from the store today."

"You did?" Jack asked and looked at Cory.

"Yes, sir," Cory answered. He looked across the table at Connie and realized she must have seen him looking at the card. "A Mr. Smithers?"

A smile spread across Jack's face. "Ol' Smitty boy!" he laughed. "I haven't seen him since high school. We used to hang together all the time. How is he? What'd he want?"

"I guess he's okay," Cory answered and started to feel the butterflies in his stomach come to life. "He asked me if I wanted a job delivering newspapers to make some extra money for Christmas," Cory said swiftly, wanting to get it all out before Jack had a chance to stop him.

"Really?" Jack asked and looked at Cory. "Do you think you can handle it? It's a big responsibility."

"I'm fourteen. I can do it."

"And can you keep up your chores here as well as your grades at school?"

"I can." Cory answered and kept nodding his head.

"Well," Jack said and took a deep breath. "Then I guess you should give Smitty a call after dinner and let him know."

"Thank you," Cory said. The butterflies vanished and Cory felt excited.

The next four months seemed to pass overnight. Cory worked hard to make sure he didn't give his step-father any reason to change his mind about the newspaper route. By the end of October, Cory had saved up quite a bit of money, more than he'd ever had before. He sat on his bed counting and recounting it.

"So, how much have you earned?" Jack asked from the

doorway.

Cory jumped and nearly launched the bills into the air.

"I have a little over two hundred dollars. Some people gave me a tip," he answered.

"That's great. I knew you could do it. So, what are you planning to buy Connie and Kyle?"

"I was thinking about a banjo I saw at the pawnshop for Connie. For Kyle I was thinking about that racetrack he's been asking about. I noticed that the toy store uptown was having a sale."

"Good," Jack nodded. "That's real good."

"What do you want for Christmas?" Cory asked.

Jack looked as if he'd been caught off guard. "Nothing. I don't need anything. You should save your money for yourself."

Before Cory could say another word, Jack walked into his bedroom and closed the door.

The first weekend in December, after finishing his paper route, Cory rode his bike uptown to do some Christmas shopping. His first stop would be the pawnshop to get the banjo. He parked his bike outside the front door and went inside.

The pawnshop smelled old and musty, like the upstairs of his Grandma Martin's old house. An old leather trunk, three small wooden tables and a rocking chair crowded the front of the store. While he waited for the clerk to finish with his customer, Cory paced up and down the aisles pretending to look at the shelves of used pots and pans, mismatched dishes and several strange figurines and knick-knacks, things people decided they could part with for a few extra bucks. On the wall behind the glass display counter hung various musical instruments, from guitars to clarinets to tubas.

"May I help you?" the clerk behind the counter asked looking directly at Cory.

"Yes." Cory stepped forward. "I'd like to buy the banjo that was in the window."

"Ah, good choice," the clerk nodded. "But I'm afraid I sold it just this morning."

"You did?" Cory said feeling disappointment seep into every bit of him.

"'Fraid so. What about a guitar? I can make you a good deal on one of these beauties?"

"No. She really wanted a banjo."

"Oh, it was for a special girl?" The clerk eyed Cory.

"For my sister."

"I see. Well, I'm sorry kid."

"Thanks anyway." Cory left the shop and returned to his bicycle. *Now what can I get her?*

All the way to Ghepetto's Toys Cory thought and thought about what Connie would like but nothing seemed right.

He parked his bike again and went inside.

"Hey, Cory, haven't seen you in a long time. How've you been?" the old clerk behind the counter greeted him.

"Busy. I got a paper route this summer and with school and all, I'm really busy."

"That's good because idle hands are the Devil's tools or something like that," he chuckled. "So, what brings you in?"

"I'm looking for the race track you have on sale. I want to get it for Kyle."

"Oh, I'm afraid I sold my last one yesterday. Could I give you a raincheck?"

"A—what's that?"

"I can take your name and number and give you a call when I get more in. I should be getting them after the new year."

"No, I was hoping to give it to him for Christmas." Again Cory felt himself slipping into feeling sorry for himself. Nothing seemed to be working out.

"Hey, what about a train set?" the old man asked.

"Nah, he's got one already."

"How about a skateboard? I've got lots of those. I could give you a discount seeing it's for your brother and Christmas."

Cory thought about it. He remembered one of Kyle's friends had a skateboard.

"Sure," he answered.

After picking out a wide board with a bright blue stripe down the center and matching blue wheels he brought it up to the counter. The clerk gave him a generous discount as promised and Cory left the store feeling better; but he still didn't have anything for Connie.

The next stop for him was the ceramic shop. Even though Jack had said he didn't want anything, Cory didn't feel right not getting him something. After giving it a lot of thought, he finally settled on getting him a beer stein. He placed a special order with the owner, Mrs. Woodard. She had been a friend of Cory's mom and checked in on them from time to time.

"Hi Cory," she greeted him when he walked into the dusty shop.

"Hi," Cory answered.

"Uh-oh, why the sad face? What's wrong?" she asked in a motherly tone.

"Do you ever have one of those days where nothing seems to be working out?"

"Do I ever!" Mrs. Woodard laughed. "Honey, look around at this stuff. Until it's fired it's extremely fragile. There are days when everything I touch seems to crumble. But what's bothering you?"

"I saved up to get Connie a banjo I'd seen in the pawnshop window but it's gone now, and the racetrack I wanted for Kyle is sold out."

"I see. So, do you have a backup plan?"

"I bought Kyle a skateboard but I can't figure out what to get Connie. Girls are hard to shop for."

Mrs. Woodard laughed. In her bib apron, with her grey hair pulled up in a bun on the top of her head and her rosy cheeks, Cory thought she would make a great Mrs. Claus.

"Well, I'm sure if you think hard enough you'll figure something out. You have a couple weeks before the big day."

"True." Cory agreed. "So, is the stein ready?" he asked and braced himself for more bad news.

"It's ready and it turned out beautifully. I'll just go in back and get it."

"Oh, thank-you," Cory said and gave a relieved sigh.

While he waited he walked around the shop looking

but not touching any of the greenware. There were ceramic Christmas trees, Santa Clauses and other assorted decorations. There were piggy banks, teddy bear banks and monkey banks. On another shelf there were plates, canisters and cups. Everything Cory could imagine, it seemed it was there.

"Here you go." Mrs. Woodard announced when she returned to the counter. She set the stein down on the counter by the cash register. "What do you think?"

Cory looked at the sixteen-inch tall stein, hand painted with a German pub scene all around it. "It's beautiful," he breathed.

"And what about the inscription?" she asked and picked up the stein and turned it over so Cory could read it.

"To Sir, with love, your son, Cory. Merry Christmas," he read out loud. "It's perfect."

"I'm glad you like it. I have just the box for it and I'll even wrap it up for you, no extra charge."

"Thank-you," Cory said. He pulled out the wad of money from his pocket and began counting.

Mrs. Woodard watched him. "Your father must be very proud of you," she said.

Cory just looked at her. He didn't know what to say. How he longed to hear those words from Jack, but no matter how hard he worked or wished it, he never did.

"Here you go," he said and handed her the exact amount.

She rang up the charges and gave him his receipt. While she placed the stein in the gift box, she noticed the large skateboard box beside Cory.

"Dear," she asked. "How are you going to get all of this home?"

Cory looked at his purchases. "Oh, I can manage," he said. "I have my bike."

"Oh no," she said and shook her head. "I tell you what, it's almost lunchtime, so why don't I just close up a bit early and give you a ride home? After all, this stein is fragile and if you were to drop it, it would break. I'm afraid I wouldn't be able to have another one ready in time for Christmas."

Cory thought for a moment. "That would be great. As long as you're sure it wouldn't be too much trouble."

"Oh, no trouble at all," she answered, reaching around her back and untying her apron strings. "Let me grab my purse and we'll be on our way."

The clock in the entry chimed twelve noon when Cory walked into the house. His arms were loaded with his two purchases. Carefully he closed the front door and hurried up the stairs to his bedroom. He hid his gifts on the shelf in his closet and then rushed down to the kitchen to start lunch.

"Hi Cory," Connie greeted when she walked into the kitchen. "Where've you been all morning?"

"Oh, I had some shopping to do." Cory answered. He took the leftover turkey and dressing out of the refrigerator. "Why?"

"No reason," Connie shrugged and sat down at the kitchen table to watch Cory make sandwiches.

"Where's Sir?" Cory asked.

"Why do you call dad that?" she asked.

Cory froze for a moment. He frantically tried to come up with a reason without breaking his promise to his mother.

"He asked me to," he finally answered.

"Well, he and Kyle went over to Grandma Martin's." Connie said.

Cory looked up at her. "When are they gonna be back?"

"He didn't say." Connie answered. "Is that for me?"

"Yes," Cory nodded.

"No cranberry sauce for me." She made a face as though she had bit into a lemon.

Cory laughed at his sister and scraped the cranberry sauce off her sandwich. "Why didn't you go with them?"

"I wasn't invited," Connie answered. "You know, it's funny. Dad seems to pick on you, ignore me, and favor Kyle. Sometimes I wonder if we are even his kids the way he treats us."

A shiver ran up Cory's spine and he looked at Connie. "Why would you say such a thing?" he asked.

"Just talking," Connie said, shrugging her shoulders and taking the milk carton out of the refrigerator. She poured herself a glass.

"Here you go." Cory handed her the sandwich on a plate. "Oh and here's a napkin."

"Thanks."

Cory fixed himself a sandwich and joined Connie at the kitchen table.

"Christmas is coming," he said.

"Duh," Connie answered and took a bite of her

sandwich.

"So, what do you want?"

Connie gave him a confused look. "I already told dad. Why do you want to know?"

"No reason. Just curious, I guess."

"Well, I want a banjo."

"Other than that?"

Connie shrugged her shoulders. "I don't know. Becky next door has a stereo. If I don't get a banjo, that would be nice."

Cory thought for a moment. Stereos were a cost a bit more than he had saved up. Maybe if he put off getting himself a new pair of Levi's he could swing it. He remembered seeing a Panasonic stereo in the pawnshop. They finished their rest of their lunch in silence.

While Cory cleaned up, Connie went next door to see Becky. He left her a note and put it on the table in case she came home and he wasn't back. He grabbed his bicycle and rode into town to the pawnshop.

Returning home, he stashed the box and made sure the coast was clear before sneaking it upstairs to his bedroom. There stereo cost more than Cory figured, taking every sent of the money he had left and leaving him nothing to buy wrapping paper with. He used the last of the saved paper from last year to wrap the skateboard. Grabbing the Sunday comics from the recycle bin, he settled down to wrap Connie's present.

"What're you doing?" came a deep voice from behind him.

Cory jumped and turned around while he knelt on the

floor. "Hi, Sir," he said and quickly stood up.

Jack walked into the bedroom and looked at the stereo box.

"What's this?"

"It's Connie's present."

"I thought you said you were getting a banjo?"

"I was, but someone already bought it. So, I asked Connie what else she wanted and she said a stereo."

"Shouldn't you have cleared it with me first?"

Cory was dumbstruck. It never occurred to him to ask permission. He stood looking down at the stereo and looked down at the box.

"What's that?" Jack asked and pointed to the odd shaped package on the bed.

"It's a skateboard for Kyle. They were out of racetracks."

"Well, seems like everyone beat you to it. Since you have achieved what you set out to, buy Connie and Kyle gifts for Christmas, you'll be needing to use the phone I suppose?"

"The phone?" Cory repeated a bit confused.

"Yes. You need to call Smitty and tell him you're quitting, effective immediately."

"But-" Cory started to protest.

Jack held up his hand again. "That was the agreement. You have the gifts. The job is over. I don't want to hear another word about it."

"Yes, Sir," Cory nodded. He waited until his step-father was gone before he sat down on his bed. Feelings of disappointment and resentment welled up deep inside of him, but one look at his gifts and they waned. Although his hopes of a new pair of jeans that fit were gone, it would be worth it to see the smiles on Connie's and Kyle's faces when they opened his gifts. He could make do with the Goodwill pair a while longer.

Christmas Eve came quickly. For the first time since his mother's death, Cory was excited about the holiday. He didn't even mind staying up to clean up the mess left by Jack's friends after their card game and drinking party. The clock on the wall said two o'clock in the morning when Cory put away the last of the cleaned dishes and headed up the stairs to his bedroom.

Just one more thing to do before he went to bed; he opened his closet and quietly took the three gifts from the shelf. He tiptoed his way down the hall past Connie's bedroom and then past Kyle's. He set the gifts under the Christmas tree and stood back to admire them. Even though they weren't in pretty Christmas wrapping paper like the other gifts around them, Cory thought they looked beautiful. He went back to his bedroom and climbed into his bed. He stared at the ceiling, too excited to sleep. But eventually sleep did come.

The sun shone brightly through the window above his bed and woke Cory from his sleep. He looked at his alarm clock. It was almost noon! He had overslept! He leapt from his bed and quickly grabbed his robe. While he hurried down the stairs, he could hear laughter coming from the living room and the sound of a banjo being strummed. He hesitated on the steps for a second and then rushed the rest of the way into the living room.

"Why didn't anyone wake me?" he asked while he stood under the arch. He looked at his sister and his mouth dropped open. Connie sat on the sofa under the living room window holding a banjo. The case lay on the floor by her feet. Immediately he recognized it.

"Cory," she beamed. "Look what Dad bought me."

"Wow," Cory forced a smile. He turned to see what Kyle and Jack were busy doing on the floor in the corner opposite the Christmas tree.

"Watch out!" Jack snapped at Cory.

"Cory look! I got a race track for Christmas." Kyle beamed.

"Wow," Cory forced a smile. "I thought they were out of them?"

"You gotta shop early," Jack answered without looking up.

Cory looked around the room. The unwrapped skateboard was shoved aside under the end table by the sofa. The stereo was still unopened at Connie's feet. He smiled.

"Aren't you going to open your present?" Cory asked her.

"In a minute. I want to play with this for a while," she answered and continued to look at the music book and adjust her finders on the neck of the banjo.

Cory looked under the Christmas tree. There was one package left. The gift he bought Jack. He picked it up and took it over to him.

"Aren't you going to open your gift, Sir?" Cory asked and held out the present to him.

"Hand me that box over there," Jack said and raised his hand to point.

Suddenly everything went into slow motion. Jack's hand hit the corner of the present and the box slipped from Cory's hands. Cory lunged and tried to catch it, but it was too late. The package hit the floor and the sound of the stein shattering inside caused everyone to look up.

Cory's entire body trembled and he clenched his fists at his side. "You did that on purpose!" he shouted at Jack. "I hate you!"

Cory didn't see Jack stand up. All he knew was he was lying on the floor in the foyer, his left cheek and eye burning in pain and Jack was standing over him.

"Come on big man, stand up!" Jack taunted. "You think you're man enough to yell at me! Stand up!"

Cory held his cheek and looked up at his step-father through tear filled eyes.

Suddenly, he was hoisted to his feet and thrown into the living room. He fell over the back of the sofa and landed on the floor in front of the Christmas tree. His head struck the floor, hard.

"Dad!" Connie screamed. "Please, stop." She rushed over and stood in front of Jack. "Please," she pleaded. "It's Christmas."

Jack glanced over at Kyle who sat frozen in shock. At that instant, his rage seemed to drain away. He turned back to Cory. "Don't you ever raise your voice to me again!" he warned and pointed his finger sharply at Cory. Then he turned and went over to Kyle and gave him a hug.

Cory slowly sat up, picked up the dented green box,

and held it to his chest. He looked around the room, tears filling his eyes.

Slowly Cory tore off the wrapping paper and then opened the box. The stein was shattered into several pieces. He picked up a large piece that appeared to be the bottom of the stein. He glanced at the inscription.

"Let me see that," Jack said and held out his hand.

Cory looked at Jack. He handed the shard to him.

Jack turned it over and looked at the inscription. The corners of his mouth turned down. He handed the piece back to Cory. "Go throw it in the garbage can," he said in a softer tone.

"Yes, Sir," Cory nodded. He turned around to head for the back door in the kitchen.

"Don't worry about making breakfast for us," Jack called after Cory. "Grandma Martin made us some French toast when she and Grandpa stopped by this morning. You should probably get started cleaning the kitchen, though. They're coming back around three."

Cory paused and looked at the boxes in his living room. This was more sharing than he intended to do; yet, at the same time he knew he needed to tell her. Katherine needed an explanation. She deserved one. Still, he couldn't bring himself to look at her.

"That was the worst Christmas I ever had. Sir had told me the night before to take the turkey out of the freezer to let it thaw. So, while they played in the living room, I started preparing the turkey. When Grandma and Grandpa Martin showed up, they invited everyone over to their house for dinner. Since the turkey was already in the oven, Sir told me I was to say behind. They would bring me home a plate."

"Cory, that's awful," Katherine gasped.

Cory stole a quick glance at his best friend. She was wiping tears from her cheeks. Cory felt bad that he had made her cry.

"So, did they bring you dinner?" she asked.

Cory shook his head. "No. Sir claimed to have forgotten or there wasn't anything left. I can't remember but I do remember Grandma gave Kyle and Connie each twenty dollars. I asked Sir if Grandma gave him something for me. All he said was, 'Now why would she do that?'

"I sat in my bedroom that night feeling sorry for myself, I guess. I was only fourteen, a kid. Christmas was for kids, at least that's what I heard the grown-ups say all the time. Anyway, Connie must have heard me. She came into my room to console me but only made it worse. She didn't even mention the stereo.

"I was never so happy to have Christmas over."

"I bet," Katherine interjected.

"The next day Kyle and Connie wanted to go to town to spend their money. Sir told me to go with them and make sure they didn't spend it all on candy. The second we walked through the door, they both took off in opposite directions. I didn't know who to follow. So, I just started walking around looking at stuff.

"I spotted a small typewriter and stood there daydreaming about the stories I could write using it."

"Cory?" a familiar voice called to him.

Cory jumped and pulled his hands away from touching the typewriter keys. He thrust them into his coat pockets.

"Hi Auntie Ag," he greeted his aunt but kept his head turned away from her.

"Cory?" she repeated. "What's the matter?"

"Nothin'."

"Ah, there is too," she said and gently turned his face toward her. "Oh my god!" she gasped when she saw his blackened eye and bruised cheek. "What happened?"

"Nothing," Cory answered.

"Did that bastard do this to you?"

"It was my fault," Cory said nervously. "I was upset and I yelled at him."

"No, it was *not* your fault!" Agnes said. "I have a good mind to call the police."

"No!" Cory shouted in panic. He grabbed onto his aunt's arm. "Please, no."

"But honey, he can't do this to you and get away with it." Agnes tried to explain. "This is criminal. It's abuse."

"It's okay, really." Cory pleaded. "Please, don't tell."

Agnes looked into Cory's eyes. Her pursed lips relaxed. "Why on earth not?"

"I promised Mom," Cory answered.

"What?" Agnes asked and cocked her head.

"The day before she died, Mama told me that Sir was not my father or Connie's. She made me promise not to tell Connie and to take care of the family, keep them together. So don't you see, I have to. I promised. If you call the police, then Connie is bound to find out about Sir. I can't do that to her. I can't turn her world upside down like mine. I just can't."

"Oh, Cory," Agnes sighed and hugged him. "Your mother wouldn't have wanted this, surely you know that."

Cory did not hug her back. He stood with his hands to his sides to afraid to move.

"Hey," Agnes smiled sympathetically looking into his pained eyes. "What do you say I buy you a late Christmas present? How about that typewriter you were admiring?"

"Really?" Cory's face lit up.

"Yes, really," she laughed. She reached up and started to take a box off the shelf.

"No, wait," Cory reached out and stopped her. "You better not. Sir will be upset if he sees it and I wouldn't be allowed to keep it anyway." The smile had vanished from Cory's face. "Thanks anyway, Auntie Ag. I appreciate that you wanted to."

"Cory," she sighed and shook her head.

He watched her dig in her purse and pull out her fist.

"Here," she tucked what felt like paper into the pocket of his jacket. He quickly pulled it out and looked at it.

"A hundred dollars!" he gasped. "No, I can't—"

"Yes you can. Spend it or hide it somewhere safe. But use it for yourself," she insisted and shoved his hand back onto his pocket.

"If it weren't for running into her that day, I don't know what I would have done." Cory said while he continued to stare at the boxes in his living room. "I was pretty low."

"Oh my god, Cory, I had no idea," Katherine said sounding stunned.

"How could you? I've never told anyone about this," Cory answered. He looked above the fireplace at the shadow left on the wall from the large portrait that had hung there.

"But why? Why didn't you let your aunt help you?"

"I don't know." Cory answered. "I guess because I still believed that underneath Sir's harsh demeanor, there was still a part of him that loved me and wanted to be my dad."

"Cory, honey," Katherine's voice sounded very maternal, gentle, full of understanding and compassion. "That's not love."

A tear fell from Cory's brown eyes and he closed them. "I know that now, but as a boy growing up in that house, I needed desperately to believe it. Honestly, Kathy, I would've put up with anything, and I mean anything, to hear him say 'I love you' or 'I'm proud of you' or even for him to call me his son again; but, that's not the sickest part," he said and looked at her through his tear filled eyes. "I'd still do anything today to hear those words from him."

Katherine's eyes filled with tears. "Oh, Cory," she sighed and reached over, placing her hand tenderly on his cheek.

Cory gave her a slight smile. "I know, it's crazy," he said and shrugged. "I hate him so much but, at the same time, he's the only father I have known.

"Kathy, you are such a wonderful woman, you deserve someone far better than me; someone who can give you all of the love and honesty you need and deserve. I'm not the right person for you. I'm such a mess inside. I don't even know who I really am anymore. Can you understand that?"

Katherine bit her lip but tried to manage a smile. She nodded silently.

"That doesn't mean I don't love you. When you asked me to marry you, I was so happy. I thought I could do it. But the more time passed, the more memories came rushing back, and the more I realized how much I had lied to you. I'm so sorry." Cory continued. "I hope in time we can be friends again."

Katherine smiled. "Don't be silly. We will always be friends."

She opened her arms and the two hugged each other tightly.

"Thank you," Cory said softly in her ear.

"I do have another question," Katherine said as they parted and returned to their separate ends of the sofa. "Why do you have to move back to— where was that again? Forest Grove?"

"Yes, Forest Grove," Cory nodded. "It's a small town just west of Portland, Oregon."

"I see," Katherine nodded. "But, why?"

"I have to go back and face my past," Cory answered. "Stop running away."

Just then, the front doorbell rang. Cory looked at his watch.

"Oh my god!" he gasped. "The movers are here already and I have to get to the airport." He jumped to his feet. "Could you toss these out. There's a garbage bag in the kitchen. Oh, and wash out the coffee pot too, please?"

"Sure," Katherine agreed.

"I'll let the movers in so they can get started. Then I have to change my clothes and get ready to go to the airport." Cory said with a sense of urgency.

He ran into the foyer and opened the front door. "Hi," he said, smiling at the two, young college students. "Right in here. I've packed everything up already and labeled the boxes. Please, be extra careful of the boxes marked fragile. I think I padded them well enough, but it wouldn't hurt to go easy with them."

"We will, Mister Martin. Don't worry," the tall, young man said.

"I'm going to go get changed and be right back down," Cory added. "If you need anything, just ask Miss Griswold in the kitchen."

When Cory reached the top of the stairs, the cell phone in his pocket rang. He took it out and looked at the screen. He recognized Connie's number.

CHAPTER FOUR

I can't believe he's really gone. It's strange. Somehow, I always thought that next to God, parents and little brothers never died. They would always be there. Yet, here I am, sitting on a plane with all of these noisy, happy, blissfully unaware people, going home to say good-bye. It's not right.

Cory continued to stare through the small window at the top of the clouds. He wasn't really looking at anything. He just didn't want to let the chatty woman seated next to him see the tears in his eyes. He didn't want to answer a lot of questions. He wanted to be left alone with his thoughts, his memories.

The garbage bags felt heavier than usual, Cory thought, while he carried them outside to the garbage can. Kyle's high school graduation party was even bigger than Connie's. More guests, more presents—bigger presents—a new computer and a shiny red Mustang convertible outdid

Connie's two-piece luggage set and charm bracelet.

"Hey, Cory. Can I talk to ya' a second?"

"Sure, Kyle." Cory dropped the garbage bags into the can and replaced the lid. Wiping his hands on his jeans he walked out to the curb where Kyle stood admiring his gift. "What's on your mind?" he asked.

Kyle turned around to face him.

"I know I haven't always been the best little brother," Kyle said quietly. "In fact, over the years, there were several times when I was an outright brat."

"It's okay."

"No, please, let me finish," Kyle said. "I've never said it before, but I do appreciate everything you've done for me, all of the cooking, cleaning, helping me with my homework, everything. No one could ask for a nicer brother."

"Well, you're welcome." Cory said and smiled to hide his confusion about this seemingly sudden change in his brother. He turned around and started to leave.

"Cory, I'm aware of how Dad has treated you over the years," Kyle said a bit louder.

Cory stopped and turned around. "What do you mean?" he asked. Kyle took a step closer.

"No birthday parties or presents, not even a cake," Kyle answered. "No Christmas gifts. Dad wasn't working the day of your graduation." Kyle shook his head in disgust. "He just didn't go, that's all. When Connie and I asked if we could go after you had already left, he forbade us. You didn't even get to have a party or any friends over."

"It's okay. That was a long time ago," Cory said and

gave a slight shrug.

"No it wasn't! It was four years ago and it's not okay, Cory." Kyle shook his head. "Can I ask you a question?"

"Sure." Cory's voice cracked as his throat tighten.

"Why didn't you leave when you had the chance? When Auntie Ag offered to set you up in your own apartment in San Francisco after you graduated?"

Cory's mouth dropped open in shock. He wasn't aware that Kyle knew about her offer. He looked back at the house, at the windows; to be sure no one had been lurking about and overheard what Kyle had just said. He took two steps closer to his brother so he wouldn't have to speak so loud.

"I couldn't do it," Cory said softly, fighting back the tears that welled up in his eyes. "I couldn't leave you and Connie here alone with Sir. Someone had to look after the two of you." He looked at his hands and swallowed hard to try to suppress the lump that rose in his throat. "I also gave my word in promise to Mom the day before she died."

"You did?" Kyle eyes widened and his mouth gaped.

Cory could only nod in answer.

"Well, now that Connie's married and I'm heading off to Oregon State in the fall, you can leave this place," Kyle said. "You can have a life of your own now."

Cory looked at the house again. "Where would I go, Kyle?"

"Portland, San Francisco, anywhere but here," Kyle suggested. "God knows I intend to get out of here as soon as I'm through with college."

"I'm glad to hear that," Cory said. He smiled, though

inside his heart was breaking. For the past ten years Kyle and Connie had been his life.

"Promise me something, Cory," Kyle said. "Promise me you won't stay here after I leave. You deserve to be happy."

Cory looked into his brother's eyes. This was a side of Kyle he had never seen. "I'll be okay."

"Cory, you have to get out of here," Kyle pleaded. "I can't leave you here alone with Dad. Not the way he treats you."

"I'll think about it."

Kyle shook his head. "It's not right," he said. "Cory, I've never told anyone this before, but at night, when I was alone in my room, I used to cry because of the way Dad treated you. You remember the day Mom died?"

Cory nodded.

"Dad gave me a watch, remember?" Kyle continued.

Cory tightened his jaw, forcing his emotions not to get the better of him. He didn't answer.

"When I saw the look in your eyes, I knew it wasn't mine. So, after dinner I put it back in the box and hid it so Dad wouldn't find it." He reached through the driver's door window and took an old, tattered, yellowed-white box off the seat. "Here, this belongs to you." He handed the box to Cory.

Tears welled up in Cory's eyes and streamed down his cheeks. He took the box, his hands shaking, and carefully opened it. He stared at the watch and then closed the box up. Without warning he threw his arms around Kyle and hugged him.

"Thank-you," he whispered into his brother's ear.
"I do love you, Cory."

"Excuse me, sir."

The words hit Cory's ears and jolted him out of his thoughts. He turned sharply and looked at the flight attendant.

"I'm sorry," she apologized. "I only wanted to know if you'd like something to drink?"

As quickly as Cory's anger flared, it was gone. "Oh," he said and looked at the cart in the narrow aisle. "Yes, I would like some decaf with some non-dairy creamer, if you have it."

"Sure," she answered and smiled. "I'll be right back." She hurried to the front galley between first class and coach.

Cory watched her whispering to the male flight attendant while she poured his coffee. The attendant looked at Cory. Their eyes met briefly. Cory turned away and looked back through the window.

The plane had found a clearing and Cory could see the land below. They were passing Mt. Shasta. It's peak was covered in snow.

"Mister Martin," a gentleman's voice said.

Cory turned to look at the male flight attendant. He was of an average height, with a thin build. His light brown hair had a touch of gray at the temples but his face still appeared youthful. His hazel-green eyes seemed as though they were reading Cory's mind.

"Yes?" said Cory while he shifted uncomfortably in his

seat.

"Perhaps you'd be more comfortable up front," the flight attendant invited and looked around the cabin at the noisy passengers. "Please, come with me."

Though Cory was confused, he stood up and excused himself as he brushed past the lady seated beside him. He quickly collected his carry-on bags from the overhead compartment and made his way up the aisle. The cabin fell silent behind him which made him feel more self-conscious.

"Here, let me help you with that," the attendant said. Taking Cory's small suitcase he put it in the compartment between the first class and coach cabins. "Please, go ahead and sit anywhere you like," he instructed.

"Why? What's this all about?"

"I noticed you seemed upset about something. The flight attendant said she thought you were crying?"

"It's nothing," Cory said feeling slightly embarrassed. "This really isn't necessary. I should go back—"

"Too late. You're bag's already stowed. It's quieter up here. Please, have a seat."

Cory hesitated and looked at the attendant. Living in San Francisco, he wasn't naïve when it came to gay men. He had worked with several before his writing career took off. Still there was something about this man that made him uncomfortable. Cory sat down in the seat furthest away from the other first class passengers.

"Better?" the attendant asked.

Cory nodded. The leather seats did feel less cramped and better padded.

"My name is Lucas Bryant, but you can call me, Luke." the flight attendant held out his hand.

"I'm Cory." He shook Luke's hand politely and started to let go, but Luke held on. Cory looked at Luke, into his eyes.

"I'm sorry," Luke apologized and released his grip.

"It's okay," Cory said to erase the awkwardness.

"I'll be right back with your coffee."

Cory settled back in his new seat and fastened his seatbelt. He took a glance through the window. The view was the same. His mind was once again being pulled to a memory of Kyle.

"Here you go," Luke said and held out a teacup made of China.

Cory looked around for the tray table.

"It's in the arm," Luke said. With his free hand, he flipped the arm of the seat open and pulled out the tray table. "There." He set the cup and saucer down.

"Thank you," Cory said. His hand shook slightly while he took a sip.

"So, do you live in Portland?" Luke asked. He sat on the arm of the seat in front of Cory and leaned against the back.

"No." Cory answered. "I'm actually between homes right now. I just bought a home on five acres outside of Forest Grove near Gaston." He looked away.

"You don't seem very excited about it."

Cory looked back at Luke. "I got some bad news just before I left."

"Hope it wasn't too bad."

Cory nodded and looked back out the window. Silently he wished the flight attendant would leave him alone.

"I see," Luke said sounding sympathetic. "Well, I have a condo in the Pearl in downtown Portland. I share it with three other flight attendants. I couldn't see getting a place of my own since I wouldn't see it very often, being in the air most of the time."

Cory bit his tongue. Luke was not going to let him alone. He took another sip of his coffee.

"Yeah, I suppose you have a point there." Cory said. "I grew up in Forest Grove, but about ten years ago, I moved to San Francisco."

"Wow, that's quite a change. So, why are you moving back? Oh, I'm sorry. That's none of my business," Luke apologized.

Cory hesitated for a moment while he eyed Luke. He had been wanting to talk to someone about it since he had received the news. He couldn't tell Katherine and there was no way he was going to tell Connie or Pamela, not now, not after hearing about Kyle. He looked at the coffee in his cup.

"A few months ago, I had a check-up and received some rather disturbing news from my doctor. So, I thought it was time to move back and be closer to my family."

"Disturbing news?" Luke's expression changed to serious concern. "Bad news, if I may be so bold as to ask?"

Cory looked into Luke's eyes again. For reasons he couldn't explain, he felt at ease talking to this man. Perhaps it was because Luke was a stranger.

"I have a thoracic aortic aneurysm," Cory started to explain. "The specialists at Saint Mary's in San Francisco said without an operation, I'd have maybe a year tops before the aorta gives out."

"Oh, Cory, that's awful."

"It's not all that bad." Cory smiled faintly. "My doctor has referred me to a specialist who works at the Oregon Health Science University on the hill in Portland. I have an appointment to see him in a couple days. I guess he's been very successful with cases like mine."

Luke's face suddenly brightened. "Hey, that's good news. So, I take it your family still lives in Forest Grove? Are they going to be there?"

"No." Cory answered. "I haven't told them. I was going to wait until I could do it in person, but—" Cory quickly turned and looked away, his eyes starting to burn again.

"The bad news you heard before boarding?"

Cory looked back and nodded. "My brother was killed yesterday."

"Oh my," Luke gasped. He looked as uncomfortable as Cory.

"He was a policeman. Who ever thought that in sleepy Forest Grove something like this would happen? None of us did."

"I'm so sorry."

"Flight attendants, please begin preparing for our landing." The Captain's voice crackled over the loud speakers throughout the cabin. "Ladies and gentlemen, we are beginning our descent into the Rose City. The outside temperature is a brisk fifty-nine degrees with scattered showers and wind gusts out of the east. We should be landing in approximately twenty minutes."

"I guess that means back to work for me," Luke said. He took the coffee cup and saucer from Cory.

"It was nice talking with you," Cory said politely.

"I enjoyed it, too." Luke said. He nodded slowly and returned to his chores.

The aircraft touched down with a slight bump and then the entire cabin began to shimmy as the plane screeched to a slow speed along the landing strip. Cory exhaled and relaxed. There were two things about flying he hated, the take-off and the landing. He attributed it to watching too many disaster movies when he was younger.

When the airplane finally stopped at the gate and the Captain turned off the seatbelt light, Cory unbuckled his seatbelt and stood up. He stretched first and then retrieved his bags.

"I want to thank you again for letting me sit up here," he said to Luke while he waited to depart.

"Oh, any time." Luke smiled. "Here, if you ever want to talk. I'll be around for a couple weeks. I need a vacation, so…" he said with a bit of a smile. He slipped a napkin into the pocket of Cory's sport coat.

"Thanks," Cory said, not really knowing what to say.

CHAPTER FIVE

Connie was waiting for Cory just outside the security checkpoint stations where she said she would be. She hadn't spotted him, but he saw her. He paused behind a large concrete pillar to stem the flood of emotion that threatened to engulf him. Seeing her made it all too real.

The crowd of arriving passengers began to thin while they passed in front of Cory making their way to the lobby. Cory waited a moment longer.

"Mr. Martin, is everything okay?"

Cory looked up. Luke was passing by with the other members of the flight crew.

"Yes," he answered. "Just catching my breath."

Luke winked and mouthed the words, call me, while he continued on his way.

Cory shook off his thoughts and braced himself for what was going to be an emotional reunion.

A smile slowly spread over his lips when he saw Connie wearing the large, white, sun hat from her wedding. She had insisted on wearing it so he could spot her easier. "Since you haven't sent me a picture of you in the last ten years," she reminded him. "I'm not sure I'd recognize you."

It was true, he hadn't sent any photographs or even a selfie. A couple times he tried taking one but didn't like the way it made him look and he felt stupid and slightly embarrassed doing it. Those pics were quickly erased from his phone.

"Cory!" Connie shouted in a tone that sounded both excited and pained.

Cory rushed to her and wrapped his arms around her. His mind slipped into another memory.

The reception hall's lights were dimmed to allow the gardenia scented candles to create the right ambiance. Connie had insisted on having three jar candles placed in the center of each table. "Candles are so romantic," she had said. Cory went along with it but wondered if the scent from sixty burning candles would overpower the church's hall. If it had, no one complained or mentioned it.

Cory carried the tray of deli meats to the buffet table. He set it on the cloth-covered pedestal.

"Where do you want these?" one of the bridesmaids asked, holding out a basket of sandwich rolls.

"Right there," Cory answered. "Take the empty basket back to the kitchen, please."

"Sure," the young woman said and smiled at him.

Cory felt a nudge from behind. He turned around to

see Kyle, his arm draped over his girlfriend Pamela's shoulders.

"I think she's kind of likes you," Kyle whispered.

"Who?" Cory asked.

"Tina," Kyle answered.

Cory turned to look at the bridesmaid right when she disappeared into the kitchen.

"You're nuts," Cory scoffed.

"Am I? I don't see the other girls helping you out with all of this."

Cory glanced at the buffet table and then back at his brother. "She's just being nice. Don't go playing matchmaker."

Kyle laughed. "You could do worse, just sayin'."

"Well, why don't you go mingle or whatever it is you two do, just sayin'." Cory teased back.

Kyle kissed Pamela's cheek and then guided her though the crowd that was beginning to gather around the dancefloor.

Cory started for the kitchen but the sound of Connie's favorite song caused him to stop and turn back. Over the top the crowd, he glimpsed Connie and Mark in the center of the floor. Their first dance had begun.

Cory had mixed emotions. He was happy for his sister. She was finally free. However, at the same time, he was sad because it meant she would moving out, leaving him. Over the past ten years since their mother had died, they had become close. They were more than siblings, they were best friends. Connie was the only one who looked out for him as best she could when it came to Sir.

He spotted Kyle snuggling with Pamela, while they watched the dance. He couldn't help but wonder how long before they would get married. *Then I will get on with my life*, Cory thought. He took the empty tray from the buffet table and headed for the kitchen.

"Excuse me, are you Cory Martin?" a man asked.

Cory stopped and turned around. He had never seen the young man before so he assumed he must be a member of his new brother-in-law's family.

"Yes," Cory answered.

"Is that your father?" The man pointed at the bar across the room.

Immediately Cory spotted Jack. He appeared to be getting a bit too close to the woman beside him.

"Yes. I'll take care of it." Cory said. He set the tray down on a nearby chair and rushed to the bar.

"How 'bout you and me getting out of this place?" Jack slurred while he spoke and leaned a bit too close to the woman's face.

"Sir," Cory said and took hold of Jack's arm. "Let's go."

"Wha—" Jack turned and saw Cory. He yanked his arm free and splashed his drink all over the woman.

She let out a scream that Cory hoped the music would drown out. The last thing he wanted was to have Connie's wedding ruined. This was her and her new husband Mark's special day.

No such luck. The woman's husband rushed over, a drink in one hand. He took one look at his wife who was busy dabbing the front of her dress and then at Cory who was apologizing.

"Just what do you think you're doing with my wife?"

"I'm so sorry," Cory said quietly, trying to keep everyone calm. He handed another napkin to the woman who kept lamenting about her dress.

"Get your hands off my wife," the man growled.

Cory looked at him and suddenly fell backward against the bar, striking his head on the way down.

"No! No! No!" the woman began screaming.

Cory sat on the floor, dazed. His left eye and cheek stung and the back of his head hurt. There was blood. Suddenly he felt himself being hoisted up off the floor.

He looked at the two men on either side of him who had ahold of his arms.

"It wasn't him," the woman told her husband. "It was his father."

The man took his wife by her arm and led her away.

"Here, hold this under your nose and tilt your head back," the man on Cory's right said and handed him a cold damp bar cloth. "Let's get you cleaned up."

"But—" Cory looked around at the crowd. "Where's—"

"Come on," the man again said. He led Cory into the men's room. "Stand here. Lean against the wall if you need to."

Cory looked at his reflection in the mirror over the sink. His left eye was already beginning to swell. Blood from his nose was smeared on his cheek and soaking the small cloth.

"Here, let me have a look," the man said. He took hold

of Cory's hand and slowly lowered it and the cloth away from Cory's nose. He nodded. "It doesn't appear to be broken but you'll have a nasty black eye for a few days."

"You a doctor?" Cory asked.

"No. A nurse practitioner," the man answered.

"What's your name?"

"Jacob. Jacob Unger," he answered. "Mark's brother."

"Oh," Cory said.

"My dad throws a mean punch."

"That was your dad?" Cory said.

"Yeah," Jacob answered. He rinsed the cloth out and then carefully wiped Cory's cheek. "Sorry about that."

"You don't have to apologize. My—Sir, was at fault. He's had a little too much to drink."

"Well, my dad isn't exactly a saint himself. He's quite the hothead especially after throwing back a few. Quick with the fists and slow with the questions. Maybe that's why I can't stand the stuff."

"I hear that."

"Well, well, well, what do we have here?" Jack asked while he held the restroom door open. "Two little faggots."

Before Jacob could say a word, Cory rushed to his step-father.

"Sir, please," he pleaded. "Let me take you home."

"I'm not going anywhere with you, homo!" Jack slurred and yanked his arm free from Cory's grasp.

"Sir!" Cory lowered the tone of his voice and grit his teeth. "You are going home, now."

Jack looked at Cory and then looked at Jacob. "Fine," he said.

"I'm really sorry about this," Cory said to Jacob.

"Don't worry about it. I've been called worse by people who matter more."

The comment took Cory by surprise.

"Cory! You're crushing my ribs," Connie groaned, jolting him back to the present.

He drew back and looked at his sister.

"I'm sorry," he apologized.

"Forget about it," Connie said, wiping his tears away. "I've been crying all week."

"Well, you still look wonderful," Cory said, forcing a smile.

"You're just saying that because you're my brother," Connie teased. She stepped back and looked Cory up and down. "Well, you've changed."

"I have?" Cory asked. "How?"

"For starters, your hair has a touch of gray it didn't before."

"Well, I am thirty-five now."

"Oh my!" Connie playfully gasped and recoiled. "You're such an old man! Should I get one of those wheelchairs for you? Are you sure you can walk? It's quite a distance to the car—"

"Very funny, sis," Cory said. "I've been thinking of coloring it."

"Oh, don't," she protested and stroked his temples. "I think it makes you look more distinguished."

"That'll be the day." Cory smirked and rolled his eyes.

"And you've lost some weight," Connie said taking his

laptop bag from him and starting to walk across the lobby toward the escalators. "Is this all you brought?"

"Yes," he answered.

"Well, we can go straight to the car then." Connie turned away from the escalators and toward the revolving door.

Cory took a last look at the main lobby. It hadn't changed much in the last ten years. A few signs were different but the carpet still looked the same, though new. A cluster of flight attendants were standing away from the lines of travelers talking and laughing a bit too loud. Cory spotted Luke and for a moment they looked at each other.

"Who's that?" Connie.

"Wha—" Cory asked.

"The person you were smiling at."

"Just a flight attendant," Cory said and shrugged. "He let me sit in first class. So where'd you park?" They passed through the slowly revolving door.

"Over there." Connie pointed at the high-rise parking lot across the skybridge. "I thought we should stop by dad's, just to check on him."

Cory stopped. "Is she still there?"

Connie gave him a look that told him she was.

"Come on, it'll be okay."

Sitting in the front passenger seat of Connie's red Subaru Forester, Cory became lost in his head.

The house was quiet. Jack had gone out for the evening, as he had done regularly since Kyle started college the last fall, leaving Cory alone. Cory didn't mind. It gave him time to work on his novel. Sitting at the dining room table with his laptop he was engrossed in his story. It wasn't until he heard the shrill squeal of a woman's laugh that he realized how late it was and that Jack was home.

The couple stumbled into the dining room and froze. Their eyes locked on Cory who was scrambling to close his laptop and gather his things.

"Thought you'd be in bed," Jack said. It was obvious to Cory that Sir was drunk.

"Didn't realize how late it was," Cory answered. He glanced at the woman holding onto his step-father's arm. She seemed more hooker than looker, ratted hair, heavy eyeshadow and dark lipstick. Her clothes looked too tight to be comfortable. In all, she was a step down from the other women Jack had brought home. "Good night," Cory said and slipped past them into the foyer.

Climbing the stairs he heard them whispering and giggling like school children. Cory shook his head and reminded himself that she'd be gone in the morning.

The alarm on his nightstand beeped. Cory awoke with a start. It felt as though he had just closed his eyes. He sat up on the edge of his bed and yawned. A loud noise downstairs brought Cory to his feet. He grabbed his robe and went to investigate.

The sound had come from the kitchen. Cory heard Jack's deep voice but not what he was saying. The sound of a pan crashing to the floor gave Cory a start when he entered.

Cory noticed the refrigerator door open.

"I can't find the bacon," the woman from the night

before said and stood up. "Oh!" she shrieked.

"Sir?" Cory said looking at Jack who was standing over the stove.

"Where's the bacon?" Jack demanded.

"We're out. I was going to pick up some on my way home from work tonight."

Jack grit his teeth and slammed his fist down on the counter beside the range. "Damn it!"

"There's sausage—"

"I don't want sausage. I wanted bacon. Why didn't you get it last night when you said you would?"

"I was held up at work."

"At the library?" Jack scoffed. "I'll tell you what the problem is, it's that damned laptop of yours. Ever since you bought that thing you've been letting everything around here go."

"That's not true."

Before the words were completely out of his mouth, Cory was hurled backward into the wall. His jaw stung and his vision was blurred.

"Don't you ever call me a liar again!" Jack spat.

"I didn't," Cory said and pushed away from the wall. He glared at his step-father which only appeared to make Jack angrier.

"Don't even think about it."

"It's okay, babe," the woman said and closed the refrigerator door. "Let's go out for breakfast."

"Whatever you want, sugar," Jack smiled at her. He then looked over at Cory. "You can clean up this mess."

"Cory?" Connie said sharply.

"What?" he answered and looked at her.

"Is everything all right?"

"Yeah. Why?"

"You haven't said a word since we left the airport. What's got you so quiet?"

"Nothing. Just thinking."

"About…" Connie pried while she continued to drive west the Banfield into town.

"About the first time I saw Stella," Cory answered.

"Oh, that." Connie shook her head. "Well, not much has changed."

"Did expect it would. Did they ever get married?"

"No," Connie answered sounding a bit perplexed. "I asked Dad about it and he just said they are still exploring their relationship or something like that."

"After twelve years?"

"I don't know. I thought it was our generation who were supposed to be the non-committal ones."

"You forget, Sir's from the hippy generation. The ones who started all of this shacking up stuff."

"Dad?"

"Yep."

"Well, I think there's something else going on with her. He won't tell me but something's definitely fishy."

Cory could hear the hostility in his sister's tone. At least they still agreed on that, their mutual dislike of Stella. However he was sure that his reasons were different from hers.

"Of course," Connie shrugged. "There's something you should know, and I know that you won't ask so I'll just tell you anyway. Dad is drinking again."

"You mean he stopped?"

"Yes," Connie answered. "He stopped for nearly three years after the doctors told him he had to quit because it was damaging his liver and jeopardizing his health."

"Wow. Who would have that that would motivate him to drop the bottle."

"Come on, Cory, be nice. Dad is really taking this hard."

"I know. I mean, I figured he would be."

"You did? Why?"

Cory caught her glance. Suddenly he felt panicked. He'd said too much.

"Kyle was his favorite. We both knew that."

"Yeah, I know," Connie agreed. She glanced in her mirrors and then moved over to take the Sunset Highway exit off the 405 freeway. "The way he's carrying on, one would think Kyle was his only child."

Cory felt a jolt as though the seat were electrified. His pulse quickened. He looked out of the corner of his eyes at Connie fearing that she may have noticed his reaction. She was concentrating on staying in her lane while they passed through the tunnel.

"I've always loved this tunnel," he said and changed the subject. "It's the Lost Horizon tunnel. You remember that old movie? The blizzard on one end and Shangri La on the other."

"Yes," Connie answered. Cory noticed her smile.

"Here we have the concrete of Portland on one side and then the green trees and forest on the other," Cory continued his explanation. "So, what's changed?"

"Remember the Candy Basket!"

"Do I ever. Tell me it's still there."

"Yes, it is."

"Oh man, Mister Vig must be ancient by now."

"Actually," Connie said. Cory heard the hesitation in her voice. "He passed away two years ago. His grandson, Todd, runs the store now as part of a chain of chocolate shops. He has a store in Northwest Portland, one in Gresham and another at the coast somewhere. You remember Todd, don't you?"

"Yeah," Cory nodded. Images of his chubby, toe-headed school chum with a runny nose flashed in his mind. The memory of it caused Cory to gag. "Who would have thought."

"True. You should see him now. He's quite the hunk."

"You mean chunk."

"No, he's slimmed down, outgrown his allergies and his quite handsome."

"You're kidding, right?"

"Nope. You've been gone a long time, Cory." Connie said, slowing while they exited the Sunset just north of Forest Grove. "People have changed."

"Some of them," Cory said and felt his stomach tighten. "I seriously doubt Sir and Stella have changed."

"Give them a chance. We're older now. We have our own lives. They can't hurt us."

"Whatever…"

"You know, I hate it when you say that." Connie's tone was sharp.

"I'm sorry. It's just that I can't forget—"

"Try. You know, they're not sitting around brooding about you, or me for that matter. Why should we waste our life on stewing over them?"

"You've got a point."

Connie turned down their childhood street. Not much had changed except that the trees were taller, some of the houses were in need of a fresh coat of paint and others a bit of repair. All in all, it was the same old neighborhood. Cory felt his stomach twist into a knot.

Connie parked against the curb and turned the engine off.

"Here we are," she announced though it wasn't necessary.

"Yeah, there it is." Cory had thought about this moment over the years but each time, each scenario in his mind didn't end well. He turned toward his sister. "What makes you think Sir wants to see me?"

Connie looked away. She stared at the steering wheel. "Actually, he doesn't," she murmured.

"What?" Cory nearly shouted at her. "Did he say that?"

"No, not in so many words."

"What exactly did he say?"

"He said you shouldn't be told at all." Connie whispered so quietly Cory wasn't sure he heard her correctly. "He said when you left, you gave up any rights and any part you had in this family."

"That figures!" Cory said and looked at the house. "So why are we here?"

"Because I think you two need to see each other."

"Why? He told you himself he doesn't want—"

"He doesn't know what he wants and for once this is what *I* want, god damn it."

Cory was taken aback by his sister's sharp tone. He looked at her. Her hands were gripping the steering wheel so tight they were shaking. He could tell she was clenching her jaw. Tears were streaming down her cheeks.

"I'm—"

"Don't!" she snapped at him.

"Okay," Cory said. "So, what do you want from me?"

"I want you to try to get along with Dad and Stella for these next few days."

"Me get along—" Cory nearly shrieked. "Connie, that's not fair. I've done nothing but try for years."

"That was a long time ago. This is now."

Cory looked at his sister in silence. She didn't know everything. She didn't know that after he moved to San Francisco he had written Sir almost daily for two months, only to have all his letters come back marked, 'Return to Sender.' She didn't know that every birthday present and Christmas gift he sent Sir back torn up or broken. Neither did she know how many of his telephone calls to Sir went unanswered. No, this time it was Sir's turn to put forth the effort.

"Okay, I try," Cory relented.

"Do more than try, Cory. Dad is hurting."

"And we're not?"

Connie lowered her brow and pursed her lips.

"Oh, all right, fine, I will stay calm."

"Thank you." Connie said and let go of the steering wheel. She started to open her door.

"Connie, wait!"

"Wait? Why?" she asked sitting back and looking at him.

"There's something I need to know. How did it happen?" Cory asked.

Connie shut her door and took a deep breath. She stared at the dashboard in front of her. "I told you everything on the phone. The five of us were having our annual get-together on your birthday at Kyle's. Kyle had forgotten to pick up the ice cream for Pam's dessert. So, after dinner he ran to the Sentry Market on Pacific Avenue, just down the street from their house. While he was talking to the clerk, a fifteen year old son-of-a-bitch with a gun tried to rob the store."

"I know that, but what happened. How did he get shot?"

"The kid aimed his gun at the clerk and when Kyle tried to disarm him, the gun went off and—" Connie turned away from Cory.

Cory put his hand on her shoulder..

"I'm okay," Connie said and wiped her face with her hands. "The kid took off and the clerk called for help. The EMT's did everything they could. Isn't that the standard answer for when things don't turn out?"

Cory didn't answer.

"Anyway, I can't be doing this," she said, again wiping

her tears away. "I have to be strong for Pam. She's having a rough time. When she saw the police captain at the door, she dropped the hot pie. The peach filling splattered her bare legs and burned her pretty bad."

"Oh no," Cory murmured and looked through the window at the driveway while he remembered.

"Cory?" Kyle whispered, knocking lightly on the bedroom door. "You still awake?" he asked and peered into the darkness of the small bedroom.

Cory turned over onto his back. "Yes," he yawned. "What time is it?"

"It's about two in the morning," Kyle whispered and stepped into the bedroom. "I need to talk to you."

"Is everything okay?" Cory asked, sitting up and leaning against the headboard of his bed.

"Everything is better than okay. It's wonderful," Kyle beamed and spun around in the darkness. "She said, 'Yes!'"

"Wha- oh my god! You asked her!" Cory was suddenly wide-awake and grinning with excitement for his brother. "She said, yes!"

"Sh-h-h!" Kyle hushed him. "Not so loud. I don't want to wake up Dad and Stella. I don't want any of them to know."

"Oh, sorry," Cory whispered.

"What're you doing this weekend?" Kyle asked. He sat down for on the foot of Cory's bed but then jumped up quickly. He started to pace.

"Nothing, why?"

"Because Pam and I want you to be our best man.

We're flying down to Vegas and getting married right away."

"But why not wait and have a family wedding?"

"And have it turn out like Connie's? No way," Kyle shook his head. "I love this girl too much to subject her to that."

"I see your point. You do know Sir's going to flip when he finds out. Are you ready for that?"

"Actually, Dad is going to flip when he finds out I quit college. I've been accepted into the police academy." Kyle admitted.

"What?" Cory gasped. "When? Why?"

"I've been thinking about it for a long time. So, I sent in an application and I was accepted at the academy beginning next month."

"But a cop?"

"Why not? They make a pretty decent living."

"But it's dangerous."

"Since when have I been afraid of danger? Remember last summer when I went skydiving? Or, how about the summer before that, racing cars in the amateur speed show in Portland? Being a cop will give me the chance to do some good and make a difference in peoples' lives."

"Wow, I guess my little brother has grown up to be a pretty neat guy. I'd be honored to be your best man."

"Thanks, Cory." Kyle leaned over and gave him a hug. "I'll let you get back to sleep."

"As if that's going to happen!" Cory laughed.

"Remember, mum's the word." Kyle looked back before he left the room.

Cory nodded, too late for Kyle to see.

The following Monday morning, Cory, Kyle and Pamela were laughing while they made their way up the front walk to the house. On the flight back from Las Vegas, Pamela kept staring at her diamond ring, and Kyle kept staring at her, kissing her every chance he could. Cory almost asked to be moved to a different seat.

Suddenly they all froze when they saw Jack and Stella standing on the front porch.

"And just where have you two been?" Jack asked.

Cory looked at Kyle and then at Pamela.

"We were—"

"I'm not speaking to you," Jack snapped.

"I'm sorry, Sir." Cory apologized.

"We went to Las Vegas. Pam got married," Kyle answered in a sharp tone and put his arm protectively around his new bride.

"Why, is she pregnant?" Jack asked.

Cory saw Kyle's hands tighten into fists. Evidently, so did Jack.

"So, you think you are man enough?" Jack said and puffed out his chest and doubling up his fists.

"Kyle, let it go," Cory stepped in front of his brother and put his hand on Kyle's shoulder. "It's not worth it." It took a few seconds but Cory felt Kyle relax.

"I'll let that one go," Kyle said to Jack.

"So just where do you two plan on living? In the dorm at college?" Jack continued with his questions.

Cory looked at Stella. He noticed she was holding a letter and a torn envelope in her hand. It looked like the letter from the police academy that Kyle had shown him. He glanced at his brother who evidently saw it too.

"Been snooping around my bedroom again, Stella?" Kyle snapped angrily.

"Leave her out of this," Jack said and took the letter.

"You already know I dropped out of college and am entering the police academy, so you can stop the games."

Jack's chest began to heave as he took in deliberate, deep breaths. "No one under my roof is going to be a stinking cop! I forbid it!"

"I'm not a child you can order around any longer!" Kyle answered him back.

"Fine. You can pack your things and get out of my house immediately!" Jack ordered.

"Wait a second," Cory interrupted. His heartbeat sped up when he remembered the promise he made to his mother to keep the family together.

"What?" Jack said and glared at Cory. "You want to say something about…" He glanced over his shoulder at the house and then back at Cory almost as if challenging him to say it.

Cory looked at Kyle and then back at Jack.

"It's fine, Cory. We weren't planning on living here anyway," Kyle said. "Wait here, honey," he said and gave Pamela a quick peck on the cheek.

Kyle walked up to Jack. "Drinking already?" he said. "I'll take my letter, if you don't mind."

Jack handed it over.

"I'll get my things and then we'll be gone. I never want to see your face again, Sir," Kyle said.

Jack's entire body tensed at the sound of that word. He stumbled back out of his son's way as if Kyle had pushed him, but Kyle hadn't.

Kyle walked up to Stella who was blocking the door. "Excuse me," he said.

Stella quickly stepped aside allowing Kyle to enter the house.

Cory stood beside Pamela. He put his arm protectively around her shoulders. She was trembling while her eyes were fixed her new father-in-law.

"This is all your fault," Jack hissed weakly at Cory.

Cory looked at his step-father.

"I should have thrown you out of this house a long time ago!" The anger came back into his voice. Jack disappeared into the house.

"I'm sorry you had to see that," Cory said to Pamela.

"It's okay," Pamela breathed. "I know how volatile Jack can be especially when he's been drinking. Kyle and I have—"

"Here!" Jack's voice thundered when he returned to the front porch with a sheet bundled up like Santa Claus' bag of toys. In one swift movement he heaved the bundle onto the lawn. When it hit, its contents spilled out.

Cory's mouth dropped open as he recognized his clothes and the things from his desk.

"What are you doing?" he yelled and rushed to grab his things. His thoughts focused on finding his laptop.

"You can get out too!" Jack answered.

Cory's anger flared. He jumped to his feet, fists clenched. "What—"

"Don't worry, Cory, I've got it," Kyle said while he brushed past his father. He held out the laptop. "I wasn't about to let him touch it."

Cory grabbed his computer and looked it over to make sure it wasn't damaged. He glared at Jack. He wanted to tell him it was his house and that if anyone was leaving it was Jack and Stella, but he remembered his promise.

"Come on, Cory," Kyle said. "You can stay with us."

CHAPTER SIX

"There's something else you need to know before we go inside," Connie said pulling Cory out of his memories and back into the car.

Cory looked at his sister and frowned. "Now what?"

"Dad doesn't know that Pam's pregnant."

"What? How could he not know? She's what, six months along?"

"I know," Connie agreed. "But she and Kyle haven't spoken to Dad since you left ten years ago."

"You're serious? Kyle hasn't talked to Sir at all?" Cory cocked his head in disbelief.

"As far as Pam knows. That's what she said."

Cory glanced at the house again. "What about you? Have you seen him?"

"Yes," she admitted. "From to time to time I've stopped by to make sure he's doing okay. He always asks about Kyle. I just tell him he's fine and drop it."

"Interesting." Cory said.

"What's that supposed to mean?"

"Nothing. Just thinking out loud."

"Well, someone has to check on him."

"I know and I'm not upset with you about it. I'm glad in a way that you do look in on him."

"There's more you should know."

"Why am I not surprised," Cory said and chuckled to himself.

"You can't say anything to Dad, but the night Kyle died, Pam told Mark and me that Kyle was so adamant about not letting Dad know about the baby, they intended to move to Seattle."

"Oh my God." Cory sank back into the seat. He never realized how serious things had become in his absence. "Okay, I won't say a word. If Pam wants him to know, then she'll have to tell him."

"Good," Connie said. "Well, let's go."

Cory opened the car door and stepped out onto the damp, grassy parking strip between the street and the sidewalk. He shut the door and quickly jumped onto the sidewalk. He stood for a moment and looked at the old two-story house where he had spent the majority of his life. It hardly looked like the same place. It was so much smaller than he remembered and not as well kept as when he had lived there. The front lawn needed mowing; the shrubs and trees needed pruning. The house itself was in dire need of repair and a fresh coat of paint.

Carefully Cory followed Connie up the narrow, cracked and crumbling walk. It was a lot to take in.

"Doesn't he do anything around here?"

"Cory, remember you promised." Connie turned around and gave him the look that said he had best not forget.

"I know."

The homemade screen door, a recent addition but hardly an improvement, opened and a little, blonde-haired, blue-eyed boy in a furry tiger costume came running out. "Mama!" he smiled and held up his arms to Connie.

"Is this Byron?" Cory asked, smiling at the four-year old boy.

"Yep. This is my baby." Connie beamed proudly, scooping him up into her arms. "Only he's not such a baby anymore."

"I can't believe how big he is. He's grown a lot since that last picture you sent me."

"Tell me," Connie groaned.

Byron wrapped his arms around her neck and put his head on her shoulder. His eyes were fixed on Cory in a blank stare. Connie turned slightly to present him to Cory.

"Say hi to your Uncle Cory."

Byron didn't utter a sound.

"Byron," Connie said and held him back to look into his eyes. "Say, hi."

Byron smiled and ducked.

"Oh, you're impossible," Connie said.

That made him smile. He wrapped his arms around her neck again and hugged her.

"He's such a phony," Connie said and laughed. "He's not really shy. This is just an act. Give him a day or two and he'll be talking your ears off."

Cory just smiled.

"Are you ready to go inside?" Connie asked and looked at Cory again.

"As ready as I'll ever be," he answered and tried to suppress the anxiety building inside of him. "Let's get this over with." He flashed a smile at her just to put her mind at ease.

When Connie opened the door, Cory was struck by an odor that made him gag. He quickly covered his nose and mouth. "What's that smell?"

"Stella is pickling garlic and boiled eggs this week." Connie rolled her eyes.

"Oh my God," Cory whispered.

"Don't worry, you'll get used to it in a few seconds," Connie said.

"I don't think so."

Cory followed Connie into the foyer. He stayed back and peeked into the living room. It was the same as he remembered. The sofa and chairs were the same, though a bit worn.

"Oh brother," Cory groaned. Books, too many for the bookshelves, were in stacks on the floor, tops of the television, end tables and coffee table.

"Stella claims she's read every one of them," Connie whispered.

"I call B.S. She's a hoarder plain and simple." Cory said while he picked one up. He showed Connie that the spine was not cracked, the tell-tale sign it's been opened.

Across the fireplace mantle and wherever there was a

clear square inch of room sat vases of flowers. Sympathy cards were proudly displayed around the room as though they were holiday greetings.

"Why does she do that?" Cory whispered while he leaned closer to Connie's ear. When their mother died, Jack wanted nothing to do with the sympathy mail. He kept a shoebox by his chair. After opening the cards and letters and removing any money in them, he dropped the unread letters and cards into the box. Then one day, he tossed the box into the fire and stood, poker in hand, while he watched them all burn.

"Stella must be in the kitchen," Connie said.

"Good."

"Cory!" Connie snapped in a disapproving tone only a mother could master.

"Oh, she couldn't hear me."

"I thought I heard someone come in." The familiar shrill voice descended the stairs behind them.

Cory jumped and turned around, coming face-to-face with Stella. He took a step back. The past ten years had taken a toll on her. Her once brunette hair was now streaked with gray and pulled back in a loose bun that was held in place by a foot long pencil. She wasn't as thin as he remembered; but then again, in her heavy, oversize sweater which was almost long enough to be a dress, he couldn't be sure.

"Stella," Cory said and forced a smile.

"Cody," she said with a sweet phony smile. "What an utter surprise to see you here."

"It's Cory," he said. "And why would it surprise you?

Kyle was my brother."

"Cory!" Connie whispered and elbowed him in the ribs.

Cory winced and rubbed his side.

"Well, don't just stand there come in and say hi to your dad." Stella spread her arms and ushered them into the living room.

Cory followed Connie over to the sofa. Both stood and watched Stella walk over to one of the two matching swivel recliners.

"Sit, sit!" she said while she rocked back in her chair. "So mother all about what you've been up to."

Cory shot Connie an angry look. He loathed it when Stella referred to herself as his mother. She was nothing like his mother. In fact his mother wouldn't have even been friends with a woman like her.

"Not much," Cory answered.

"Really? You haven't done anything in ten years?" Stella answered.

"Just working to make a living." Cory answered, purposely trying to be vague.

"That's not what I've heard," Stella said.

"Why am I not surprised." Cory matched her tone.

"Didn't you just buy the VanDyke's old log house and five acres on Bald Peak?"

"What?" Connie gasped and looked at him.

Cory looked at his sister. His shoulders slumped a bit. "I was going to tell you tonight at dinner."

"How— Why—"

"Later," he said to her. He looked back at Stella who

had a smug, satisfied expression.

"Hasn't it been vacant for years and run down?"

Connie jabbed Cory in the ribs again, seemingly as if she knew what he was about to say. He grit his teeth and smiled at her before taking a deep breath and relaxing again.

"Actually, I've had it completely renovated," Cory answered.

"But it's such a big house. How will you be able to keep it clean?"

"It's no bigger than this house and you seem to—"

"I can't wait to see it." Connie interrupted.

"Well, it sounds like a lot of work," Stella said, continuing to poke.

"I'm not afraid of a little housework. In fact, I'm used to it." Cory answered with a goading smile.

"It must have cost you a fortune," she said. "They were asking over half a million for it.? How will you ever afford it?"

"I had a good agent." Cory said bluntly.

"Stella, where's Mark?" Connie interrupted and changed the subject.

"He went after Pam," she answered. "She went over to the mortuary to check on the arrangements your father and I made." Stella glanced at the front door.

"What?" Cory gasped in indignation.

"And Daddy?" Connie interrupted again.

"I'm right here, sweetheart." His voice came from the foyer behind them. Jack walked around the couch, bent down and kissed Connie's cheek.

Cory's pulse quickened. He watched Jack walk across

the room to his chair and sit down. Cory felt his anger melt. Jack had aged. His once broad and strong shoulders were slumped. His arms and big hands that once inspired fear in Cory seemed weaker and smaller. He looked tired. His eyes were red and puffy from lack of sleep, crying, drinking or a bit of all three.

"How's my little tiger?" Jack asked looking at Byron.

"Grrrreat!" Byron growled and raised his hands like claws.

Jack walked over to his chair and sat down. He looked around his chair as though he were searching for something. "Oh, where's that damned TV remote?" he cursed.

"Daddy," Connie spoke softly. "Cory is here."

"I can see him!" he snapped angrily.

Connie jumped.

"I'm not blind," he added and glared at Cory before giving him a head-to-toe once over.

"Oh, for the love of Pete, would you look at that!" Jack snapped. He gestured toward the floor in front of Cory.

"What?" Cory searched the floor under his feet. Even Connie bent forward to see what was the matter.

"I just had these carpets cleaned, and you go and track mud in here. Good for nothing, ungrateful brat!"

Cory looked at his shoes. Sir was right. On the tip of his left shoe, there was a spot of mud but hardly enough to get upset about.

"I'm sorry," Cory apologized. Suddenly he felt like he was twelve years old again, afraid and nervous. "I didn't notice it. I'll take them off." He reached down and started to untie his shoes.

"Don't bother," Jack growled and looked away.

Stella stood up as though on cue. "I'll get some paper towels," she said. "While I'm in the kitchen, may I make you a drink, Cory?"

"No, thank you," Cory answered trying his best to be polite. He knew that Stella was baiting him in front of Sir.

"What's the matter?" Jack turned back toward Cory. "Afraid a good whiskey might make a man out of you, or would you prefer one of those sissy drinks?"

"Neither," Cory answered, remaining calm. "I don't drink, Sir."

"Your brother always drank with me," Jack said.

Cory looked at Connie. She shook her head as if she read his mind.

"Well, I'm sure Kyle had his reasons," Cory said.

"What's that supposed to mean?" Jack demanded.

Cory recoiled at the harshness in Jack's voice. Growing up he had heard that tone used on him a lot. Usually it was followed by a sharp slap upside his head. Suddenly the feeling of it all came terrifyingly back to him.

"Nothing, Sir," Cory answered quietly.

"Here, wipe your shoes off," Stella said and held out a torn paper towel. When Cory reached for it, she let it drop to the floor.

"Here, honey." She walked over and handed Jack a drinking glass half-full of whiskey with one ice cube.

Cory picked up the paper towel and wiped off his shoe. He glanced at Connie who seemed unusually quiet.

He assumed she would have more to say, possibly something in defense of him. She sat cradling Byron while she watched Jack. She had that motherly concerned look in her eyes.

"I think I need to get some fresh air." Cory stood up.

"Cory," Connie said. She grabbed his hand.

"Ah, let him go, Connie," Jack said and pawed at the air. "He's not worth it. On the other hand, Kyle, Kyle was a real man, not afraid of anyone or anything."

Cory looked at his step-father. He could feel his anger building inside of him.

"You really don't want to get in that conversation with me, Sir," Cory said, his jaw tightening.

For a moment, their eyes locked. Jack's hard expression softened as though he knew what Cory meant. He turned his gaze back to his drink and gulped down another mouthful.

"Ah, sit down," he said and again swatted the air.

The sound of the front screen door slamming shut caused everyone to look toward the foyer. Pamela stood beside Mark. Her eyes were red and damp with tears. They were fixed on Jack.

"You dirty son-of-a-bitch!" she screamed. She took two steps into the room and held onto the back of the couch.

Connie's mouth dropped open and her eyes widened in apparent shock.

Mark rushed over to Connie and took Byron from her.

"Come here, son," he said and held Byron protectively in his arms. "Let's go outside." The two quickly disappeared out the front door.

"What makes you think…what gives you the right to step in and take over my husband's funeral arrangements?" Pamela continued to scream at Jack.

"I have every right!" Jack yelled back at her. "He was my son long before you came along and threw yourself at him."

"Oh, you are such a pathetic, little man," Pamela said as though the words were bitter tasting in her mouth. She shook her head and clinched her fists.

"Pam," Connie spoke up. "Surely it can't be that bad."

"Oh, it's bad," Pamela said tears filling her eyes and starting to stream down her cheeks. She turned back to Jack. "Do you want to tell them what you did?"

Jack sat swirling the ice cube around in his glass.

"Daddy?" Connie looked at Jack. "What have you done?"

Jack didn't respond. He took another gulp of his drink and then looked blindly at her.

Connie turned back to Pamela.

"You coward." Pamela sneered. "I'll tell you what that son of a bitch did. He had Stella forget my name on a note giving him authority to make the decisions. He tried to have Kyle's body cremated!"

Cory suddenly went numb all over. The thought that Kyle's body would be cremated had never occurred to him. He just assumed there would be a coffin and a funeral like there was when their mother had died. The thought of not being able to say good-bye jolted him.

Connie gasped. She looked at Jack, tears flooding her

eyes. "Daddy, how could you?"

"He was shot in the head, for god's sake!" Jack yelled at her. "There's no way I wanted my son on display for people to gawk at."

"That was not your decision to make!" Pamela screamed through her tears.

Suddenly her expression changed from anger to pain. She put a hand on her round stomach. "Oh!" she gasped.

Connie jumped to her feet and rushed around the sofa to Pamela's side. "Take it easy. Breathe."

Cory stood beside Pam, letting her steady herself by holding onto his arm.

"What's the matter?" Jack asked and sat forward in his chair. He grabbed his glasses from the side table and put them on. His eyes widened when he saw Pamela's stomach. He stood up. "You're pregnant?"

"Oh, don't get excited," Pamela snapped at him. The pain had subsided and her anger returned. "I have no intention of ever letting you anywhere near this baby."

"What?" Jack pulled his head back and gave her a confused look. "Kyle would never have wanted that."

"How in the hell would you know?" Pamela seethed. "You were never a real father to him. You're just a judgmental, self-righteous, pathetic little drunk!"

"You don't know what you are talking about! You don't know me!" Jack's voice thundered.

"And you don't know me!" Pamela said flatly. "You never took the time or bothered to get to know me. You just called me a tramp, a whore. Well, I do know what Kyle wanted and he never wanted you to even know we were having this baby. He hated you so much he took a job in Seattle so we could move away before the baby was born."

"You're lying!" Jack started to turn his back on them.

"Am I? How sure are you of that?"

Cory watched Jack's entire body stiffened. He knew the look and took a step back toward the foyer, taking Pamela with him.

"If you want to know the honest truth, Kyle died hating you!" Pamela screamed.

Without warning, Jack threw his drinking glass at Pamela.

She ducked. Cory jumped out of the way. The glass hit the wall only inches from Pamela's head and shattered. Whiskey ran down the wall. Ice and glass shards exploded all around the floor.

"Get out!" Jack ordered.

"Dad," Connie pleaded.

"All of you!" he shouted.

Connie hesitated, looking first at Jack and then at Cory for help.

"Come on, sis," he said.

Cory glanced back at Jack. He collapsed back into his chair, his hands shaking and tears streaming down his cheeks. For a moment Cory remembered that look. It was the same one Jack had when Cory's mother had died. Cory wanted, as he did back then, to hug his step-father and tell him it was going to be okay but just as then, Jack wouldn't allow it.

While the three started down the walk, Mark came walking up to them.

"I think I should take Byron on home. He doesn't need to see and hear all of this."

"I'm sorry, Mark," Pamela apologized.

"Oh, no," Mark said, shaking his head and looking at the house behind them. "Dad and Stella had it coming. I'm glad you're back, Cory."

"Thank you, Mark."

"Well, I hope you're happy," Stella yelled at them from the porch. "You three have really upset your father now. Can't you see he's in pain? He has just lost his son." She turned and glared directly at Cory in an icy cold stare. "Why did you came back here? Why couldn't you have just sent flowers like any other decent human being?"

Cory let go of Pamela and glanced at Connie. He shook his head and Connie turned away.

"Really? You want to insert yourself even more into this?" Cory took a step toward Stella. She quickly stepped back. "You don't know anything about this family. Just because you spread your legs for Sir doesn't mean you're family. You're nothing but a whore."

"How dare you!" Stella shrieked.

"Cut the act, he isn't watching," Cory said and grinned. Lowering his voice he took another step toward Stella. "I've been doing a little research while I was away. Not only is Oregon not a common law state, but you're still married to a man in Sacramento. So, what are you doing here?"

Stella's mouth gaped.

"You do realize, without Sir here, you'll be back on street again. You see," he lowered his voice and glanced over his shoulder at Connie who stood at the end of the walk. "My name is the one on the deed for this house."

Stella stood on the front porch, speechless.

"By the way, I gave your husband your new address." Cory turned around and joined Connie and Pamela.

"What did you say to her?" Connie asked.

"Why?"

"I've never seen her look so frightened."

"I don't care what you said," Pamela interrupted. "It's about time someone put that bitch in her place!" She looked at Cory. "I'm so glad you're here. I wish you could stay forever."

Cory put his arm around Pamela's shoulders.

"Well, should I tell her?" he asked Connie.

Connie smiled and nodded.

"What? Tell me what?" Pamela asked.

"I am staying."

"Don't tease. My heart can't take much more," Pamela said and twisted so she could see Cory's face.

"It's true. I bought the VanDyke's old house south of town."

Pamela looked at Connie. Connie nodded.

"It's true," she said.

"That's wonderful," Pamela said and wrapped her arms around Cory.

After helping Pamela into Mark's car and waving them off, Cory took his place in the passenger seat of Connie's Subaru.

"What a welcome home," he said while he pulled the seatbelt across his chest and waist. He glanced at Connie when she didn't respond. She had tears in her eyes while she stared straight ahead. "Connie? Are you okay? What's wrong?"

"Why? Why couldn't you just let things go? You promised."

"Let things go?" Cory shook his head in disbelief. "Connie, you heard what Pam—"

"I know," Connie snapped. "I know, but couldn't you see he was hurting?"

"Stop it! Stop it right now!" Cory said. "Sir doesn't need you or Stella or anyone defending him. Hurting? We're all hurting, Connie. What he is doing now is the same thing he did when mama died. It's all about his grief, his pain. To hell with us."

"I know," Connie admitted softly. "It's just…I need him, Cory. I know that you don't. You have always been strong and after mama died you took care of us and were always there for us. When you moved away you became independent and built a life for yourself. You don't need Dad anymore but I do. I still need some bit of my past to hold onto. Can you understand that?"

Cory was silent. Yes, he understood what she was saying, but, she was wrong. He did need Jack. He did need the man he knew to be his father.

CHAPTER SEVEN

While growing up in Forest Grove, Cory never dreamt he would be staying in at the Budget Inn there. The contractor had discovered a water leak in the kitchen's plumbing but not until it damaged the new wood flooring, walls and cabinets. He had informed Cory until it was fixed, the city would not permit occupancy. So for the forcible future, his things would remain boxed up in the dining room and living room while he played tourist in a motel.

Cory's rented room was small, but comfortable. He wished he could say the same thing about the bed. He tossed and turned all night, dozing off but not really sleeping. His mind kept replaying the events from the previous day. He had been so convinced that moving back to Oregon, to be around family – Connie and Kyle – would be good for him, just what the doctor ordered; but then, the telephone rang and turned his world upside-down.

Katherine had tears in her eyes when they said their

good-byes at the airport. She begged him to let her come with him to be supportive but he assured her it would be best if she stayed in behind in San Francisco.

"We're still friends," she had said but it sounded more like a question.

"Always," Cory answered. He gave her a kiss and a hug and almost changed his mind about leaving her.

The flight to Portland was horrible. It felt like it was taking forever but talking with Luke made it better. It was the only truly enjoyable part of the day. Cory thought about the napkin in his coat pocket, but it was late.

Cory punched his pillow in an attempt to get comfortable and watched the numbers change on the digital alarm clock next to the bed. He was not looking forward to the next day and at the same time he couldn't wait until the morning. At least he wouldn't be alone with his thoughts anymore. At seven o'clock, Cory decided it was okay to shower without waking the people in the next room. Not that he really cared, they were pretty noisy themselves with the headboard banging against the wall and the sound of the woman moaning and screaming. Still, Cory felt he should wait until at least a polite hour before turning the shower on.

The morning air felt crisp when Cory stepped out of his room and onto the outdoor walkway of the second floor. He glanced over the railing to see if the rental car he ordered when he checked in the night before had been delivered. The woman at the front desk had promised that he would have it by seven in the morning.

Sure enough, it was there and by eight-thirty, Cory had

arrived at Pamela's house.

"Hi, Pam," Cory greeted when she opened the front door. "Boy I thought I had a rough night."

Pamela wrapped her arms around him and gave him a hug. Cory felt her body trembling.

"Are you okay?" he asked.

"I am now," she answered. She stepped back and let Cory enter.

Cory stepped looked around while he took off his jacket. The living room was a spotless. He looked at the dining room and noticed a small pistol like the one Kyle had told him he used for a backup.

"Pam, what's going on?" Cory asked. He pointed at the gun.

"Oh," she said. "Last night after Mark and Connie left, Dad and Stella showed up. At first I thought they were here to apologize and try to make amends but as soon as I opened the door, that cow pushed me aside and headed down the hall toward the bedrooms. Jack headed down to the basement. I ran after Stella to stop her, but she had already opened the closet and begun throwing Kyle's things onto the bed. I yelled at her to stop but it did no good. She just kept grabbing at Kyle's things. I ran to the safe in the spare bedroom and opened it. I took Kyle's backup pistol out—"

"Oh, Pam, you didn't," Cory gasped.

"No. I grabbed the telephone and called the police. By the time Dad came up out of the basement with Kyle's camping gear, Tom was here. He told them to put everything down and to leave before he arrested them for trespassing and attempted robbery."

"What did Sir do?"

"He put everything back and he and Stella left."

"I don't believe it. Just when you think he couldn't stoop any lower… What about the gun?"

"After Tom left, I took Kyle's pistol and brought it out here. I couldn't sleep. I was afraid they'd come back. I wanted something that would get their attention."

"You wouldn't really…"

"No," she answered. "I took the bullets out."

Cory didn't realize how tense he was until he felt his body relax. Ever since he witnessed Jack shoot a stray cat on his Grandma Martin's farm, Cory hated guns. He was eight years old then and seeing the poor animal die because it had the misfortune of cutting across the Martin property left an indelible impression.

"I was so afraid they would come back," Pamela continued. "I still am."

"Well, it wouldn't surprise me, but instead of the gun, keep my number handy."

Pamela looked at him and then at the pistol. "Deal. I'm so happy you've come back." She hugged him.

"When were Connie and Mark coming over?" Cory asked while he followed Pamela into the kitchen. The hearty aroma of freshly brewed coffee filled the air.

"They said they'd be over at nine. Coffee?"

"Decaf?"

"Actually half-caf, but don't tell Connie. She only likes the real stuff." Pamela laughed.

Cory watched his sister-in-law pour a cupful.

CHAPTER EIGHT

Slowly the motorcade wound its way along the narrow cemetery road. Cory looked out of the window when the limousine crested the hill. The view of the valley in the distance was amazing. The clouds parted allowing the sun's rays through. It reminded Cory of a painting he'd once seen at the Museum of Modern Art in San Francisco. It was so serene.

"I think the service went well," Connie said, breaking the silence.

Cory shifted in his seat so he could see in the three behind him.

"It was," Mark agreed. "I think Dad was on his best behavior. He seemed sober, at least."

Pamela didn't say a word.

Cory turned back around and glanced at the side mirror. He wondered what Jack and Stella were saying in the limo behind theirs.

"Let's just hope they both keep it up for another half hour," Cory said.

The limo came to a stop at the edge of the narrow road. Cory let himself out while the driver opened the back passenger door and offered his hand to Pamela. Her eyes were damp with tears.

"Thank you," she whispered to the chauffer and reached out her hand to Cory.

The four stood beside the limo while the pallbearers removed the casket from the back of the hearse. Cory glanced over his shoulder right when Jack and Stella joined the four. Slowly they followed the flag draped casket down the hillside until it came to its final resting place.

Cory took a deep breath. The air was thick with the scent of carnations and lilies. The scent brought back memories of his mother's funeral. The flowers weren't as bountiful but their scents mingled together in a sweet sickening odor.

The graveside service seemed more for the police department than it was religious. The police chief said a few words about how sad and yet how proud they are to have known Kyle, and what a loss it was not only to the entire police force, but also to them, personally. Then a lone bugler at the top of the hill played Taps. Two officers folded the flag and then presented it to Pamela. After which, the service concluded.

Cory helped Pamela to her feet. They waited until the many friends and loved ones had returned to their cars before they started back to the limousine.

"Cory," Jack called from behind them.

Cory stopped and turned around.

"May I have a word with you?" Jack asked. "Alone?"

The soft quality in Jack's voice threw Cory off guard.

"Ah, sure," he answered. He turned to Mark and Connie. "Wait for me in the limo, please?"

"Sure," Mark said and put his arm around Pamela's shoulders.

Jack walked up to Cory and waited until they were alone.

"So, what did you think of the service?" Jack said.

"It was okay. Why?"

"No reason." Jack dug his hands into the pockets of his old, black slacks. "You and Pam seem to be getting along."

"Yeah, well, she's a really nice girl."

"Good, glad to hear it."

Cory gave his step-father a curious look. "What's this all about?"

"Nothing," Jack answered and appeared to fidget a bit too much for it to be the truth.

"Really?" Cory said.

"I was just thinking that maybe, if you two hit it off then—"

"Wait a minute!" Cory stopped. "Kyle's not even buried yet and you're trying to fix up his wife?"

"No. I was just looking out for her. She's all alone and with child."

"Oh my God. That's what this is really about," Cory said with a disbelieving laugh. "This isn't about her, it's about the baby. You're afraid that Pam might marry a stranger some day and you'll never see your grandchild."

Jack looked away confirming what Cory suspected.

"No, I'm not going to marry her," Cory snapped.

"Aren't you forgetting the promise you made to your mother, to keep the family together?" Jack said quietly though in Cory's ears it sounded like he were shouting.

Cory had no answer. He watched Jack continue up the hill to where Stella was waiting by their limo. He looked at Mark and Connie consoling Pamela while they waited for him to join them.

"What was all of that about?" Mark asked when Cory joined them.

"Nothing," he answered and took his place in the front passenger seat.

The ride back to Pamela's house seemed much shorter. The driver drove at regular speeds instead of the slow processional speed. Cory had little time to process his conversation with Sir. Jack's parting words echoed louder and louder in his ears. Cory shook his head, trying to silence his memory.

The chauffeur dropped the four of them off at the curb in front of Pamela's house. Mark had offered a tip to the driver, but he refused, saying that he was an old schoolmate of Kyle's and it was his honor to help out.

"So, shall you follow us over to Dad's?" Connie asked Cory.

"I don't know," he answered. "I'll wait with Pam until her mom and sister arrive. Then I'll think about it."

"Is everything okay?" she asked, slipping her arm around his. "Ever since you and Dad talked at the cemetery, you seem preoccupied. What did he say?"

"Oh, nothing worth repeating," Cory answered.

"Well, I hope you aren't sorry you decided to move back to the area. I mean Gaston isn't Forest Grove but it's closer than California."

"No, I'm glad to be back."

"Good. Please don't leave me again." She threw her arms around his neck and gave him a tight hug.

"I won't," he said into her ear. "Not in a million years."

CHAPTER NINE

By the time Cory reached Sir's house, the street was lined with police cars. The stop off at the motel to change out of his suit had taken a bit longer than he planned due to an unexpected call from Katherine. She figured the funeral would be today and wanted to offer her condolences again and make sure he was all right. Cory parked his rental car a block away.

While he walked back to the house, Cory spotted his Aunt Agnes' Mustang. The realization that she still had it made him smile but more than that, seeing she was here gave him a sense of relief.

When Sir had thrown him out, Agnes took him in.

"Your mother left that house to you," she reminded him after picking him up. "You should have been the one doing the throwing." However, she seemed to understand and only made the comment once.

A year later, when he was considering a job transfer to

San Francisco, she helped him to get set up in his first condo. The only thing she asked in return was, if he ever published his novel, to give her a copy. When that day came, he dedicated it to her.

The house was packed. Cory inched his way through the foyer and into the living room. He spotted Stella making her rounds handing out bottles of beer and picking up the empties. Cory slipped back into the foyer before she spotted him and made his way to the kitchen.

Agnes and Connie stood at the counter with their backs toward him. The noise in the house was so loud, Cory couldn't tell if they were talking.

Right when Cory was about to speak, Agnes turned around with a plate of sandwiches in her hand.

"Cory!" She set the plate down and rushed to give him a hug. "Why haven't you been by?" she said into his ear. "Oh, never mind. I'm so glad you're here."

"Me, too," he said and kissed her cheek.

"Connie was just telling me the news, you bought the old VanDyke place."

"Yes," Cory said.

Connie gave him a kiss on the cheek while she took the Agnes' plate of sandwiches. She disappeared into the dining room.

"What about San Francisco?" Agnes asked.

"Nothing," Cory answered. "I just felt it was time to come back."

Agnes eyed him suspiciously. "We'll talk later when it's not so crazy."

"Sounds good."

"I'm so glad you're here," Agnes gushed and kissed him again.

"Is there any more salad?" Stella asked while she walked into the kitchen. "Oh! What are you doing in here?"

Cory glared at her.

"I meant in the kitchen," she explained and walked around him to retrieve a large bowl of potato salad from the counter.

"I guess I should get out of your way."

"Here." Agnes grabbed a Coke from the fridge and handed it to him.

"Thanks."

Slowly Cory wove his way through the dining room toward the living room. Even though he was upset by their conversation at the cemetery, he still felt the need to look in on Sir.

Jack was standing by the fireplace, drink in hand, talking to two men. Cory recognized them. They were Jack's old drinking buddies. Cory turned away.

"Hey, Cory." Someone shouted at him.

Cory froze. Slowly he turned around.

"I don't believe it!" one of Jack's buddies grinned. "You've really grown up since I saw you last."

"Hey, come over here an join us," Jack said and held out his hand toward Cory.

"That's okay, Sir, I was looking for Mark."

"What's the matter? You too good to have a drink with us?"

"No, that's not it."

"Then come over here."

Cory did as he was told partly out of embarrassment. The others in the living room were looking at him.

"Sir, you know I don't drink," he said, lowering his voice.

"Nonsense," Jack said. "You can at least have one last drink for your brother." He staggered forward and held a glass of whiskey and ice out in front of him.

"Kyle knows I don't drink. So I'm sure he wouldn't mind."

"Well I do," Jack shouted. He thrust the glass toward Cory's face.

Cory pulled away and started to leave. Jack grabbed him by the arm and pulled him back.

"One drink isn't gonna kill you." Again he raised the glass to Cory's face.

"Stop it!" Cory shouted and slapped the glass away, knocking it out of Jack's hand. It shattered on the brick hearth and splashed its contents on the two men standing nearby.

"Go on!" Jack shouted. "You always were a disappointment. Why couldn't it have been you? You're nothing but a gutless, little faggot! I wish you were dead!"

The next moments were clouded in anger and embarrassment. Cory's clenched fist struck his step-father in the jaw and sent Jack stumbling to the floor. A thin red ribbon of blood seeped from the corner of his mouth. He looked up at Cory.

"Get out!" he shouted. "Get out of this house and don't you ever come back again! You're dead as far as I'm concerned! Do you hear me, faggot? You're dead!"

Cory began to tremble. He looked at the shocked faces around him. He pushed through the crowd on his way to the front door.

"You're dead!" Jack's voice thundered.

The screen door slammed shut with a loud bang.

Cory ignored the curious looks of the people standing in groups on the front lawn. He headed for the sidewalk trying to think of where he parked his car.

"Cory!" a voice called to him.

Cory stopped and turned around.

"Cory," Connie called while she ran after him. "Where are you going?"

"Anywhere but here," Cory answered.

"Don't go," she pleaded. "He didn't mean it. He's drunk."

"That's the second time," Cory corrected her. "He knows exactly what he said."

"Give him another chance—"

"Another…Connie, how many chances does he get? When is it my turn for him give me a chance?"

"Cory, please," Connie pleaded. "He's just upset because of the funeral and everything that's going on. That's all."

"No, Connie," Cory said and shook his head. "It's not just the funeral. This goes all the way back to—" Cory stopped himself. "Connie, I'm glad you see some good in him. You always have. I just wish I could."

"Please, give him another chance." Connie said.

Cory took his hands out of his pockets and held them up in surrender.

"I can't," Cory said. "I'm glad you need him in your life. But I can't keep doing this to myself. It's just too much stress. I've got to get out of here."

"So, what are you going to do?" she asked.

"I don't know," Cory answered. He looked back at the house. "I just have to get away from here."

"Cory, please, don't leave."

"I have to." Cory pulled himself free from her hold on his arms. "I love you, but I can't do this. I'll call you later." He started down the sidewalk toward his car.

"Cory, please!" Connie cried.

He didn't respond. His heart was pounding in his chest. Once seated behind the steering wheel, he took several deep breaths in an attempt to calm himself before finally driving away.

CHAPTER TEN

The afternoon air had a slight chill to it. Cory turned the collar of his sport coat up against his neck while he sat on the stone bench beneath a tall fir tree. He rubbed his hands together hoping the friction would get the blood circulating and warm them. He looked down at the grey granite headstone in front of him. The yellow roses he brought lay just beneath the engraved name.

"Oh, mama," he said out loud. "I wish you were here. I wish you could help me understand why. Why did you have to do it? Why did I have to know?"

"Do you always talk to yourself?" a voice asked from behind him.

Cory jumped to his feet and turned around, nearly tripping himself. He grabbed his chest and panted.

"Don't do that!" he gasped while he looked at the man dressed in blue jeans, red T-shirt and black leather jacket. "You scared the life out of me. Hey, I know— how did you—"

"You're sister found the napkin and called me," Luke interrupted and answered. "She told me what had happened and that you would probably be here. She's very worried about you."

"Yeah, well, that's Connie for you," Cory said and turned away.

"She sounds very nice," Luke added.

"She is. She's too nice for her own good."

"I have to be honest with you." Luke stepped beside him. "I was hoping *you* would have called me."

"You were?"

"Yes." Luke nodded. His green eyes seemed to sparkle when he smiled.

"Why? You queer?" Cory asked.

Luke stepped back and looked at Cory. "I've been called worse," he answered. "But I prefer the word, gay. Why? Does that bother you?"

Cory looked at him and then down at his mother's headstone. He didn't know what to think. Everything was so confusing. Finally he looked at Luke.

"I'm sorry. I didn't mean to offend you. No, it actually doesn't bother me." Cory walked over to the bench and sat back down.

Danial followed him and sat down beside him.

"No harm, no foul," he said, "But if you were anyone else, I would have decked you for that comment." He bumped his shoulder against Cory's playfully. "So, in the light of full disclosure, how about you? Are you gay?" he asked and looked straight ahead.

No! Cory wanted to scream but something deep inside silenced him. He looked at the headstone by his feet. He thought about his mother, about Katherine and Connie.

"I don't know," Cory answered in a hoarse whisper.

"That's an honest answer." Again Luke bumped his shoulder against Cory's. "Have you ever had sex with a guy?"

Cory's breath caught. Images flashed in his head.

The house was quiet except for the radio that played softly in the kitchen while Cory finished washing the dishes. Grandma Martin had picked up Connie and Kyle for the weekend.

A burst of laughter from the living room drowned out the music from the radio.

"I'm gonna go get another beer," a man's voice announced.

Moments later one of Jack's poker buddies walked into the kitchen. Cory didn't turn to look which one. He continued to rinse the soap suds from the pizza pan.

"Someday you'll make some lucky guy a good wife," the man said.

Cory nearly dropped the pan back into the soapy water.

"Didn't mean to upset you," the man said and put his hand on Cory's back. He leaned around to get a look at Cory's face but Cory kept his head down. "You're a good kid."

The man returned to the living room and left Cory alone.

After finishing the dishes, Cory paused in the foyer.

"Is there anything more, Sir?" he asked.

Jack looked up from his cards. The air in the living room was thick with cigar smoke.

"I think this is my last hand," the man with his back to Cory said. "I need to be getting home to the little woman."

"What time is it?" Jack said and turned to see the clock above the mantle. "Oh my, it's nearly two already."

"Sir, I'm going to take a shower and then go to bed."

"Fine. Get out of here," Jack said and waved him off.

Cory retrieved a clean t-shirt and pair of underwear from his dresser and grabbed his robe before heading to the bathroom. He could hear Jack talking in the foyer below. He was telling one of his friends he could crash on the couch.

Cory put his clothes on the bathroom counter and then started the water in the shower. By the time he undressed and stepped in, the water was hot. He closed his eyes and let the water massage the tight muscles in his neck. It felt good to let his body relax.

The sound of the bathroom door opening, startled Cory out of his thoughts.

"Gotta pee," the man from the kitchen said. "Hope you don't mind. I mean, we're all guys here, right?"

Cory didn't answer. He grabbed the bar of soap and began running it over his arms and chest. A shadow grew on the shower curtain and then the man groaned while he relieved himself.

"Too much beer," he said.

Cory didn't respond. He closed his eyes and willed the

man to leave.

Suddenly the feeling that someone was behind him caused him to jump and turn around. His feet slipped on the wet surface of the tub. Before he could fall, two strong hands grabbed his arms and held him up.

Cory looked into the blue eyes of the man from the kitchen, at his tussled, sandy-blonde hair, at his tanned chest covered with light hair. Suddenly he realized the man was naked.

"It's okay, isn't it?" he whispered quietly. "I mean, we're just two guys needing to get—"

Before he finished his sentence or Cory could object, the man pulled Cory close, wrapping his arms around Cory's thin body. His mouth opened and he pressed his lips against Cory's. The hot water beat against Cory's back. The older man continued his seduction. Cory felt his body responding to the man's touch. He closed his eyes.

Everything seemed to happen in slow motion and yet quickly at the same time. Cory didn't wanted it to end but didn't. It was all so confusing. When he opened his eyes, the man was gone.

Cory shut off the water and quickly dried himself. He slipped into his clean clothes and opened the bathroom door.

Jack stood in the doorway of his bedroom. His arms folded over his chest. A cross look in his eyes.

He knows what you did, a voice in Cory's head accused him.

"I'm sorry, Sir," Cory said and slipped past his step-father into his bedroom across the hall. Closing the door behind him, he pressed his back against it.

Eventually he laid down in his bed but sleep wouldn't come. Instead, Cory kept replaying the shower scene over and over in his mind while he tried to convince himself it was just a dream.

The next morning, Cory woke to find Jack's friend gone and Jack sitting at the table as if nothing had happened.

"Earth to Cory Martin," Luke said into Cory's ear.

Cory pulled away and looked at Luke but saw the face of Jack's friend. He jumped to his feet and took a step away before the image morphed back into Luke.

"What's the matter?" Luke asked.

The moment was gone. Cory felt himself relax. He sat back down.

"Nothing," he answered.

The two sat in silence for what felt like an eternity. Cory's mind was whirling with random thoughts and unanswered questions.

"How does a person know if he's gay?" Cory asked and stared straight ahead.

Luke stood up sharply which took Cory by surprise.

"You hungry?" he asked

Cory shrugged. "Sure, I guess."

"Good, I know a place. We can leave your car here and take mine. I'll bring you back later."

"Okay," Cory answered but sounded hesitant. He stood up and the two walked back to the narrow cemetery road where their cars were parked.

"You're gonna like it," Luke said with a grin.

CHAPTER ELEVEN

Cory looked at the passing scenery while Luke drove through the streets of downtown Portland. The city hadn't changed much in the years he was absent. The trees along the sidewalks had grown and filled out nicely. There were a few new buildings but for the most part it was still recognizable.

Luke crossed Burnside into the northwest part of downtown, an area that Cory was unfamiliar with. He glanced at Luke behind the wheel. Luke didn't appear the least bit concerned or nervous. He slowed the car to a stop, parking it alongside the curb and shut off the engine.

"Well, we're here," he announced.

"Here?" Cory looked out at the antique, street lamps and narrow park. Across the street was an old brick building. A neon sign above some darkened windows flashed in lavender letters, Madam M's Burgers.

"Yep, here." Luke jumped out of the car. Cory opened

his door and did the same.

A small group of people turned the corner ahead and started toward them. Cory was used to the eccentrics in San Francisco but with last night's news of a stabbing in a Macy's men's dressing room and another attempted robbery that didn't end well, he couldn't help but feel nervous while watching the group of four, three men and one woman, draw closer.

"Evening," a man dressed in a leather jacket, with a tattoo on his neck and dark eye make-up said while they passed.

"Evening," Cory answered in a barely audible tone. He watched them until they crossed Burnside into downtown.

"What am I getting myself into?" Cory asked when Luke joined him on the sidewalk.

"Relax," Luke said. "Come on."

Cory followed Luke across the street toward the building with the neon sign.

"This place has the best hamburgers—you do like meat don't you? I mean you're not a vegan or vegetarian are you?"

"No. I like hamburgers."

"Good. This place is famous for them."

Luke pulled the heavy wooden door open and held it for Cory.

"This place isn't weird is it?"

The smile faded from Luke's lips. "Get inside before I smack you."

"Okay, okay. Just askin'" Cory said holding his hands up.

The foyer of the restaurant was striking. It reminded Cory of one of La Stazione back in San Francisco. The walls were covered in a red velvet patterned wall paper. Along the side walls were what appeared to be benches made from bed headboards. Floor lamps with fringed shades brought to mind images of early twentieth century bordellos. Suddenly Cory felt cold. He grabbed Luke's arm and stopped him from approaching the hostess station.

"What is this place?" he asked.

"What do you mean?"

"You didn't bring me to a brothel did you?"

Luke let out a laugh. "Why on earth would I do that? Besides, there haven't been any legal brothels in Portland for nearly a hundred years. Would you knock it off and relax?"

"Okay," Cory answered but still felt nervous.

"Two for dinner," Luke informed the hostess.

"Right this way."

Cory followed them into the dining room. Immediately he noticed the benches and tables appeared to be made from old brass and wooden bedframes just like those in the foyer. Antique mismatched chandeliers hung above each table. When the realization that this wasn't a whore house sank in, Cory found himself intrigued by the décor.

"Your server will be here momentarily," the hostess said while she placed two menus on the table.

"Thank you," Luke said.

When they had settled into their seats, Cory began to feel more relaxed.

"Pretty cool place," Luke said and handed a menu to

Cory.

"Yeah—"

"Oh my god!" gasped an effeminate waiter in a white shirt and black slacks. He put his hands to his cheeks and then stretched them out in anticipation of a hug. "Lucas!" he squealed and threw his arms around Luke's neck. "When did you get back in town?"

"About a week ago."

"Why haven't you been in? I'm hurt."

"I've been busy," he answered.

The waiter gave Cory the once over. "I see."

"Come on, Robin, knock it off," Luke said. "We just want to have a nice quiet dinner. No drama."

"Drama? Me? Oh po-lease," Robin scoffed. "What do you want from the bar?"

"I'll have a beer."

"I wasn't asking you. I know what you want." Robin looked at Cory.

"I'll just have a Coke."

"Pepsi okay?"

"Sure," Cory answered.

"Back in a flash."

Cory watched Robin wind his way around the other tables and into the bar area before turning back to face Luke.

"So is this a gay restaurant?"

"No, but a lot of the servers are gay." Luke answered. "While we are on the subject, you asked how a person knows if they're gay or straight."

Cory nodded.

"That's a tough question to answer. I mean, it's different from one person to the next."

"Oh," Cory said.

"Here you go," Robin said and set the drinks on the table. "Are you ready to order?"

Luke's mouth opened and he looked at Cory. "Sure, we'll take two Tillamook Cheeseburgers with fries and cole slaw on the side."

Cory nodded in agreement.

"How do you want the burger cooked?"

"Well done," Luke answered.

"Same for me," Cory added.

"Coming right up." Again Robin disappeared, this time to the kitchen.

Cory took a sip of his Pepsi and made a face, he preferred Coke. "So, if I may get a little personal, how did you know?" Cory asked.

Luke took a quick drink of his beer and then set the glass back onto the table. "I guess I always knew that I was different as far back as I can remember. At the time I didn't know what to call it, but I've always been attracted to men. I remember having a huge crush on one of my parents' friends. He was about your build but had short, red hair. I remember he had a wonderfully furry chest." Luke sighed and smiled. "But he was a truck driver, so we didn't see him too often."

Cory listened with interest, not saying a word but nodding his head while he thought about his own life.

"All through grade school, I found I was attracted to the older boys in my school. The girls were okay. I even kissed a few. But it didn't feel the same as when I looked at the boys.

"I a sophomore when you could say I lost my virginity. He was a senior and on the football team. It was only one time, but it felt so natural to me. That's when I knew I was gay.

"How about you? Have you ever been with anyone?" Luke asked.

Cory suddenly felt uncomfortable. Images of Jack's friend popped into his head. He avoided looking at Luke. "I was engaged," he answered and took another sip of his Pepsi.

"To a woman?" Luke prodded.

Cory looked back at him sharply. "Yes," he answered indignantly.

"What happened?"

"What do you mean?"

"Well, you said, was. You're not married so…what happened?"

"We called it off."

"Oh, I see," Luke said. "So, did you ever kiss her?"

"Yes," Cory answered. "We were engaged."

"So how was it, the kiss, I mean?"

"What sort of question is that?"

"Did you see fireworks? Did you feel stirrings, anything?"

Cory felt his anger rise because of being asked such a personal question. Once the initial shock wore off, Cory's anger dissipated. He started to think about how he felt when he had kissed Katherine.

"It was okay," he answered.

"Just, 'okay?'" Luke asked. His smile didn't help put Cory at ease.

"Why? What should it feel like?" he asked in a belligerent tone.

"Well, when I kissed my first boyfriend, there were stirrings. There were fireworks in my head. I wanted to hold on and not let go."

Cory felt uncomfortable. His face began to feel warm. He took a big gulp of water from his glass and nearly choked. There were no fireworks, no stirrings when he kissed Katherine. Cory became nervous.

"Let's change the subject," he said.

"I'm sorry," Luke apologized. "I wasn't trying to upset you." He reached across the table and gently put his hand on top of Cory's.

Cory quickly pulled his hand away. He nervously looked around the restaurant to be sure no one was watching. The other patrons were focused on eating and visiting with the others at their tables. No one was paying any attention to them.

"No, I'm the one who should be apologizing. I brought up the subject." Cory said quietly. "The answer to your question is, no. There were no fireworks, no stirrings."

"Why you were engaged then?"

Cory fidgeted and avoided looking at Luke. "I don't know. It's complicated."

"How so?"

"It just is, that's all."

"Here you go," Robin announced and set a plate in

front of each of them.

"Looks good," Luke said.

Robin pulled a bottle of ketchup from his apron and set it on the center of the table. "Is there anything else I can get you, besides a refill?" He picked up Cory's Pepsi glass.

"Another beer," Luke answered.

"Be right back."

Cory watched Robin walk away. He looked at the thick burger in front of him and the mountain of hearty French fries.

"There's no way I can eat all of this," he told Luke.

"They have doggie bags. You'll want to take the leftovers. They're just as good."

Cory waited for Luke to begin eating before he took a fry and tasted it. It was good. It reminded him of the fries at The Golden Gate restaurant on the Wharf. The seasoning was about the same.

Robin returned with their drinks and left them without saying a word.

"So, did you ever have sex with her?" Luke asked right when Cory took a gulp of his cola.

The question took Cory by surprise. He swallowed wrong and began choking and coughing. He looked around the dining room at the curious faces of the other diners. He looked down and continued to clear his airway.

He glanced at Luke who appeared to think it all funny.

"No!" Cory answered, his voice sounded weak.

"What about with a man? Have you ever had a man make love to you?" Luke leaned in and asked quietly.

Cory's whole body stiffened. Slowly he raised his head

and looked into Luke's hazel-green eyes. A memory came flooding back.

"Night, Cory," Angela said while she walked past the counter on her way to the front door. "See you tomorrow."

"Good night," Cory called, ignoring the "No Talking" sign above the library entrance turnstiles.

"Don't forget to lock up when I leave."

Cory grabbed the keys from under the counter. "Right behind you."

He reached the front door as it closed behind his co-worker. Impatiently he pulled the door shut and pushed the bolt up, securing it. He then turned the key in the deadbolt, locking the door. He had a few more books to finish checking in before he would be ready to leave.

He turned back toward the check-out counter when something hit the glass on the front door. Cory jumped and turned around. His heart pounded wildly. Looking at him through the glass was a familiar face. One he hadn't seen in three years. It was Sir's friend from the shower. A confusion of emotions hit Cory like a tidal wave.

"Go away, we're closed!" he yelled.

The man wouldn't leave. He put his palm against the glass.

"I need to talk to you," he said.

"We're closed." Cory repeated.

The man motioned for Cory to unlock the door.

Cory inched closer but had no intention of complying.

"Don't you remember me?" the man asked. "I'm Wes. Your father's friend."

"I know who you are. What do you want?"

"Well, I was wondering if we could go somewhere, maybe get a drink and talk?"

"Why? You don't have some disease do you?" Cory asked, part of him fearing the answer. He had heard of AIDS. He knew it was spread by unprotected sex. He wasn't that naive.

Wes laughed. "No. I'm clean."

"Well, I don't drink."

"That's okay, we could just have a Coke or something. Come on. Please?"

Cory thought for a moment. Jack had taken Kyle and Connie camping for the weekend with his sister's family. There was no reason he had to rush home. He had no excuses.

"Okay," Cory agreed. "Give me a minute to lock up and I'll meet you at the side door."

Moments later, Cory found himself in the passenger seat of Wes' car as they headed off in the dark to find an open restaurant. Cory had never been outside Forest Grove and driving in the dark, where he couldn't see anything familiar was beginning to make him nervous.

"Where are we going?" he asked.

"It looks like everything is closed around here. So, I thought we'd head into Portland." Wes answered.

"Portland?" Cory nearly shouted. "I need to get home."

"Relax. It'll be fine. We'll just have one drink and then I'll get you home." Wes assured him.

Cory turned his face toward the window. The light

from the streetlamps seemed to strobe while they sped past. Cory was already regretting accepting Wes' drink invitation.

They drove up and down the streets in downtown Portland. Wes said he knew of a place that was still open but appeared to have trouble finding it.

"This is crazy. It should be right here," he half-apologized. "Tell you what, we can grab a couple bottles of Coke and then take them back to my motel room. We can—"

"I really should be getting home."

"Why? You dad is off camping. Why spend the night alone when you could have company?"

It sounded more like a statement to Cory than a question, so he didn't answer.

Wes pulled the car into the parking lot of a motel and told Cory to wait there. Then he disappeared through a door next to a sign that read, Office.

Cory stared at the door and imagined himself getting out of the car and running, but that thought frightened him more. They had driven around crisscrossing street after street so many times Cory had lost track of where they were or how to get back to the freeway home. He reached for the door handle just as Wes came out of the office. He held up a single keycard and grinned while he walked around to the driver's door.

"We're in luck. They had a room," he said as he sat down behind the wheel.

"I thought you said you had a room."

"I do now," Wes said and pulled the car forward into a parking space across from the office.

Cory looked at the door directly in front of them. The number 17 was affixed directly above the peephole. He felt his pulse quicken.

"Come on," Wes said, opening the car door and stepping out. He unlocked the door and flipped on the lights.

Cory entered the motel room and looked around; he had never been in a motel before but had seen them on TV. Still, the room looked small, with a single queen bed, two nightstands, a small table with two chairs and a flat screen TV mounted on the wall opposite the bed. Toward the back of the room was a bathroom. Cory could see the mirror through the open door.

"This was their last room," Wes said and shut the door before locking it. "Hope you don't mind sharing the bed."

Cory didn't answer. He thought about not having his pajamas or his toothbrush or a change of clothes for the morning. He hoped Wes would take him home early enough for him to change before he had to go back to work. Angela would surely notice if he showed up wearing the same clothes from today.

"Need to use the john?" Wes asked.

Cory shook his head.

"Why don't you slip off your clothes and get in bed while I use the bathroom," Wes ordered though he tried to make it sound like a suggestion.

Cory knew it wasn't. He waited for Wes to close the bathroom door before he began to disrobe. He draped his shirt and jeans over the back of the nearest chair and then slipped between the sheets.

He shivered. His t-shirt and briefs provided little insulation against the cold sheets. He pulled the covers up around his neck and waited for the warmth of his body to heat the bed.

"Hope you're warming up that bed," Wes said when he emerged from the bathroom. He stood at the foot of the bed and kicked off his shoes while he unbuttoned his shirt. He faced Cory while he removed his shirt, tossing it on the other empty chair.

Cory remembered the sight of Wes' furry chest. He began to feel more nervous.

Wes unfastened his belt and then unbuttoned his jeans, his eyes fixed on Cory. He grinned while he unzipped his fly.

Cory looked away.

Wes' jeans hit the chair at the same moment Cory felt Wes slide under the covers beside him. Wes wrapped his arms around Cory. Cory felt Wes' body tense.

"Wouldn't you be more comfortable with those off?" he asked and snapped the waist band of Cory's briefs.

"No, I'm okay," Cory answered.

"Take them off, now." Wes' tone was firm, reminding Cory of Sir.

Cory slipped out of bed and did as he was told. Wes held the covers up so Cory could slip beneath them.

Wes put his arm around Cory and pulled him closer. Beneath the covers, Cory could feel the softness of Wes' skin against his own.

"There, isn't that better?" Wes said and began kissing Cory's shoulder, neck, and ear. He rolled over, his body pinning Cory to the mattress. He opened his mouth and kissed Cory.

"Cory?" Luke said a little louder and kicked Cory's leg under the table, jolting Cory out of his thoughts.

"What?" Cory asked.

"You okay?"

"Yes, why?"

"You were staring."

"I was?"

"Yes."

"Sorry."

"So, have you ever had a man make love to you?"

"I wouldn't call it making love," Cory answered, quietly, before he realized what he was saying.

"What?" Luke said, sounding concerned.

Cory shook his head. "I don't want to talk about it."

"You know you can trust me, don't you?" Luke said.

"I barely know you." Cory responded.

"Exactly. What have you got to lose?"

Cory stared at Luke. His mind was arguing whether or not he should say what he was thinking. Finally he picked up his Pepsi and took a sip.

"I was raped, twice by one of my step-father's friends," Cory said. He set his glass down and glanced at Luke.

Luke sat with his eyes wide and his mouth agape.

"The first time I was fifteen. He was drunk and it happened while I was taking a shower. The next time he showed up when I was closing up after work. I was eighteen this time. He said he just wanted to talk." Cory shook his head and looked away. "He took me to a motel somewhere in Portland and—God, I can't believe I was really that naïve?"

Luke waved off Robin who had come to collect the plates.

"I'm so sorry," Luke said.

"It's okay. It was a long time ago."

"It wasn't that long ago. You aren't that old, yet."

"True, but I've put it behind me."

"You're a better man than I," Luke said and emptied the last of his beer glass.

"Well, I never saw him again. I have no idea what happened to him or if he's even still around."

"Would it matter?"

"No. Not really." Cory began to stare at his uneaten burger.

"So, what are you thinking know?" Luke asked.

"I don't know," Cory said. "I guess I want to know what it all means."

"It doesn't mean anything."

"But part of me liked it." Cory admitted. "I mean, I came. Does it make me gay?"

"No." Luke shook his head.

"I'm just so confused," Cory sighed.

"I can imagine." Luke said. "Well, I can't eat another bite and you've barely touched yours. What do you say we get a couple to-go boxes and I take you back to your car?"

"Sure," Cory answered. He couldn't help but feel as if Luke regretted inviting him to dinner and was dumping him. Then he wondered why he cared.

Moments later, walking back to Luke's car with their doggie bags, Cory found himself growing nervous again.

"I bet you wish you hadn't come to see me tonight. I'm a real nut case, eh?" he said.

Luke stopped in the middle of the park beneath a tall fir tree. "No, not at all," he answered. "I'm glad you told me. I'm just sorry that all happened."

Luke smiled; his hazel green eyes sparkled in the light from the streetlamp. Cory felt warm inside. He looked at Luke.

"May I..." Luke asked and took a step closer to Cory.

"May you what?"

Slowly Luke moved closer and closer. "This."

Cory closed his eyes as their lips met and they kissed. Cory felt the back of his legs tingle and grow weak. When they parted he grabbed onto Luke for a brief moment to steady himself.

"Ever since I saw you on my flight, I wanted to do that," Luke confessed. "May I see you again?"

Cory nodded.

CHAPTER TWELVE

"Just a minute!" Cory called as he stepped from the shower of his motel room. He grabbed one of the white terrycloth towels that hung on the rack above the toilet and quickly wrapped it around his waist. He grabbed the other one to dry his hair. Before he could get out of the bathroom, there was another loud knock.

"I'm coming!" he yelled while he opened the door.

"Oh," he greeted. "It's you."

"Gee thanks," Connie said. She walked into the room and let Cory close the door. "Who were you expecting?"

"No one," he answered.

"It didn't sound like no one." She eyed him and then looked at the room. "I see you still make your bed."

"Old habits die hard, I guess."

"Well, we're adults now."

"I know." Cory walked back into the bathroom to finish toweling off.

"The bed is nice. Firm."

Cory bolted into the room. "Don't—"

Connie looked at him while she stood beside the bed. "Cory, you need to relax. Dad isn't going to check your bed."

"Whatever."

Cory grabbed his jeans from the chair where he had left them the night before and went back into the bathroom to put them on.

"So, did that flight attendant guy find you?"

Cory walked back into the room and sat down on a chair to put his socks and shoes on.

"Why did you call him?"

"You told me you talked to him on the plane and that he helped you. I thought he might be able to help me."

"Help you with what?"

"Keeping you from moving away again."

"Who said anything about moving away?"

"You did. Yesterday. You said you had to get away from here."

"Connie, I meant from Sir's."

Connie frowned. "You know, I asked dad why he told you to call him that."

"You did? What did he say?"

"He said he didn't. He said after mom died you started that on your own."

"Figures."

"Cory, I wish you could see he's not as bad as you think. Really."

"We're not doing this again."

"Cory, there are two sides to every story if you'd just stop and take a look."

"I don't have to. I lived it."

"So did I. I was there too, remember. Dad did a lot of nice things for us—"

"Name one thing he did for *me*."

"He let you get that paper route."

"He also made me quit once I used my money to buy you and Kyle presents for Christmas. And that's another thing. I told Sir I was wanting to buy you the banjo I'd seen at the pawn shop. When I went to buy it, Sir had already bought it."

"No he didn't."

"Connie, he did."

"No, Cory, he didn't. He bought my banjo from a music store in Hillsboro. I know because I had to take it in to have one of the tuners fixed and I needed the receipt."

"But I saw the case..." Cory searched his memory trying to remember. Could he have been wrong all this time?

"I know you still love him."

"What?"

"If you didn't, whatever he did or didn't do wouldn't matter to you."

"That's nuts."

"Holding onto your anger is nuts."

"What are you, a shrink?"

"No, but I see a psychologist. She's helped me deal with a lot of my feelings and issues."

"Issues? From what?"

"From losing mom and feeling guilty…" Connie looked away.

"About what?"

"About stuff. Never mind."

"No, I want to know. What stuff?"

"About telling dad about his Mr. Taylor."

Cory suddenly felt numb. He looked at his sister. "Wes? What do you mean?"

"I saw him go into the bathroom when you were showering late at night."

"So," Cory said trying to remain calm.

"I told Dad. He told me to go back to bed, but I still had to use the bathroom. So, I waited. After you went to bed, I went to the bathroom. I heard Dad and Mr. Taylor arguing downstairs. Dad threw him out and told him to never come near his children again."

"He did?"

"Yes. Did that Mr. Taylor do anything to you?"

"Let's talk about something else." Cory answered and turned away from her. He started packing his suitcase while he tried to pretend that nothing was wrong.

"Sure," Connie said. "So when will your house be ready? I want to see it."

"The inspector did his final walk through yesterday. So, once the contractor gets the approval I should be able to move in this Wednesday."

"So, are you excited?"

"Of course. I can't wait to get out of here. The room's okay. It's just that I want to get settled before…" He caught himself. "Before the bad weather hits."

"Good point," Connie said with a nod.

"Once I'm settled we can have a dinner party to celebrate."

"Dad too?" Connie asked.

Cory stopped brushing his hair. He stared at his reflection in the bathroom mirror. There was a part of him that wanted to say, yes, but the thought of it turning into a scene like the other day worried him.

"We'll see," he answered. "So, how do I look?"

"Fine," Connie answered. "There's something else I wanted to talk to you about while we're alone."

"Really? What?"

"I don't know how to say it so I'll just ask. Are you gay?"

"What?"

"I heard what Dad said, what he called you. He called you that at my wedding reception. It doesn't matter to me if you are or aren't—"

"Then why ask?"

"Because, I need to know. I don't want there to be any secrets. I mean—"

"Connie, I don't know," Cory answered trying to end the conversation.

"You mean—"

"No, I mean exactly that, I don't know and I don't want to talk about it right now."

"But—"

"Nothing. Look, Connie, if this answers your question, I was engaged in San Francisco."

"To a man?"

"No, to a girl named Katherine."

Connie's eyes suddenly widened with shock. "You were?"

"Yes. Now, can we just drop it?"

"So, is she moving up here?"

"No. We called it off."

"What? Why?"

Cory could hear the disappointment in her voice.

"We just decided we were better off being friends. Are we still meeting Pam for breakfast?"

"Yes."

"Then we should be going."

"We can take my car and leave your rental here."

"Okay."

"This conversation isn't over," Connie said while she planted a kiss on Cory's cheek and slipped out the door.

Cory locked the door behind him and hung the Do Not Disturb sign on the door. He followed Connie down to her car and then slipped into the passenger seat.

"Have you talked to Pam since the funeral?"

"Yes, briefly."

"How's she doing?"

"I don't know," Connie answered. "She didn't show up at the gathering at Dad's yesterday."

"Surely you didn't think she would after everything Sir and Stella put her through."

"I guess not," Connie answered. "I called later last night to confirm we were still on for breakfast today. She told me she sent her mother and sister home. She just wanted to be alone."

"That doesn't sound good."

"I know. I'm worried. She's taking this pretty hard."

"Well, duh, her husband was just murdered." Cory said. Suddenly a thought occurred to him. "Whatever happened to the guy who shot him?"

"The police have him in custody. They tracked him down a few hours after…"

"So, there's going to be a trial."

"Eventually. But you know how slow the legal system moves. It probably won't be for a year."

"Whatever happened to having a right to a speedy trial?"

"That's only in the movies."

"Poor Pam."

"Yeah, it's going to be hard on all of us."

"That's true," Cory agreed and looked out the window while Connie drove across town. "I still can't believe he's really gone; that he won't come walking through the door any minute with his usual impish grin. He was always up to something."

"Remember when he hid in my closet and scared the daylights out of me?"

Cory laughed. "Yeah. It took forever for his black eye to go away. Who taught you to punch like that?"

"I don't know," Connie answered. "Instinct?"

"Whatever it was, he never did that again. Hey, do you remember when his marble rolled under mom's car when we were at Grandma's? I think he was about four or five."

"Yes." Connie answered with a slight laugh. "He got in and took it out of gear and released the emergency brake.

The car rolled down the driveway and into the street."

"Where did he learn to do that? I don't even think I knew how to do that at the time and I was about ten."

"I don't know. Maybe Dad showed him? Whatever, I am still surprised that the car didn't hit any of the other cars on the street and that it stopped when it hit the curb."

"All of that for a silly marble."

They shared a laugh.

Connie pulled up to the curb and parked behind Mark's vehicle.

"Well, here we are," she announced.

Cory glanced at his cell phone.

"Missed a call?" Connie asked.

"No," Cory said and slipped it back into the pocket of his jacket.

"'Morning," Pamela greeted them with a big smile when she opened the front door. "Come in."

The house smelled of freshly brewed coffee, cooked sausages and hotcakes. Cory glanced at the dining room table when he stepped into the foyer. The table was beautifully set, like the tables in magazine ads. Covered platters of different sizes kept the food beneath warm.

"Let's just go right over to the table," Pamela said. "Would you like some coffee?"

"Sure, but I can—"

"Nonsense, you're my guest. Besides, I have to get the pancakes," Pamela said and hurried back to the kitchen. "Everyone, please have a seat."

Cory glanced at Mark and then Connie. The three walked into the dining room and took a seat. Mark pulled a chair out for Byron.

"Here," he said and lifted his son up and set him down. "Now, don't make a mess like you do at home."

Mark looked at Connie. "Did you remember to bring his bib?"

"I put it in…oh, damn. I left the bag on the kitchen table at home."

"Damn it, Connie."

"I'm sorry."

Cory watched Mark disappear into the kitchen. He looked at Connie. "Is everything okay?"

"Yes," she answered. "He's just tired. He's been working a lot of overtime these past few months. We're trying to save up to buy a house."

Mark came back carrying a dishtowel in his hand. "Here you go, buddy." He tied one end around Byron's neck and then spread the other end out covering his lap.

"I'm sorry, I forgot it," Connie whispered when Mark too a seat in the chair beside her.

"Don't worry about it," Mark said and gave her a kiss.

Cory watched the exchange and seeing they were okay, relaxed.

"Here we go." Pamela said while she walked into the dining room with a large platter piled high with more pancakes than the five of them could possibly eat. She set the platter on the table and removed the covers from the other platters.

"Pam, you've really outdone yourself," Mark said.

"I'll say," Cory agreed. "Pam, you really didn't need to do all of this."

"I don't mind," she answered, still looking at the table. "Oh, I'll be right back, I almost forgot."

Before anyone had a chance to say another word, she disappeared back into the kitchen. She returned moments later with a gravy boat filled with steaming hot maple syrup in one hand and a pot of freshly brewed coffee in the other. "I think this should do it," she said and sat down beside Cory. "Well, shall we eat?"

Cory noticed Pamela's hands tremble when she took her napkin and placed it over her stomach.

"You must have been up all night," Mark said, picking up the plate of sausages and bacon.

"I couldn't sleep. So, I had to do something."

Cory put his hand on hers. "Give yourself time."

"I guess that's all I have now," Pamela said in a sorrowful tone. "He's really gone, and no amount of wishing and praying is going to bring him back." She glanced at Connie who was pouring syrup on a pancake. "The syrup is an old family recipe."

Connie looked at her. "You made your own syrup?"

"Yes," Pamela answered sounding proud.

Connie dipped her finger into the syrup on the edge of her plate and then tasted it. "Oh my, this is better than the store bought stuff."

"Kyle thought that too. Excuse me, I'll be right back." Pamela disappeared into the kitchen again.

"I'm really worried about her," Connie whispered while she kept an eye on the kitchen doorway.

"She's fine," Mark said. "Eat."

"Well I—"

"I almost forgot your creamer," Pamela said and set the small ceramic cow on the table.

"Where did you find that?" Cory asked. "Grandma Martin had one that looked just like it."

"It should," Pamela laughed. "She gave it to us."

"That is so cool." Cory poured some cream into his coffee. "What would you like first? Eggs? Pancakes?"

"Nothing, I don't think I could eat right now." Pamela shook her head and passed the platter to Connie. "I love cooking, but I'm a hopeless nibbler. I have to sample everything while I'm cooking."

"That's too funny. I do the same thing," Cory admitted.

"Say, what are you doing tomorrow?" Pamela asked.

"Me? I actually have an appointment," Cory said hesitantly. "Why?"

"I've decided I am going to find out what the baby is."

"You are?" Connie said sounding shocked. "But I thought you wanted to be surprised?"

"I think I've had enough surprises to last me a lifetime," Pamela answered. "I just can't handle any more. I need to know. I think it would be comforting."

"So, what time will you going?" Cory asked.

"My appointment's for ten. I was hoping you'd all come with me."

"I wish I could, Pam, but I have to work," Mark said. "Connie could go with you."

"Yes, I'm free. I could leave Byron with a sitter. Then afterward, we can go by Washington Square and do some baby shopping."

"That'd be great." Pamela said.

"I really wish I could go too but my appointment is at nine and I can't change it. It's all the way in Portland."

"That's okay. Maybe we could all have dinner?"

"How about I take everyone out?" Cory offered.

"Sure," Pamela said and smiled.

The conversation shifted to Cory's new house and when he would be moving in. Everyone ate their breakfast and even Pamela nibbled on a pancake and sausage link. When everyone finished, she stood up and began to clear the table. Connie quickly jumped to her feet and took the stack of plates from her.

"Pam, please, let me take care of these. You've done more than enough for one day."

"I don't mind, really."

"No, I insist."

"Let me handle this," Mark said and stood up. "The three of you can take Byron into the living room while I clean up."

"But—"

"But nothing," Mark said. His tone was firm causing Pamela to acquiesce.

"Come on, Pam," Cory said, putting his arm around her shoulders. "Bring your orange juice and let's sit down in the living room."

"Oh, all right."

"I'll grab some coffee. You want a refill, Cory?" Connie said while she wiped Bryon's face and removed his makeshift bib.

"Sure," Cory answered.

Once he was free, Byron ran over to Pamela. She smiled at him. "If your mom says it's okay, you can go in the playroom and play Uncle Kyle's video games."

Byron looked at his mother.

"Just a minute," she said and handed Cory his coffee cup. "Okay, let's go."

"So, how's Jack?" Pamela asked but her tone belied her concern.

"I don't know. I haven't talked to him." Cory answered. "We didn't exactly part on good terms yesterday."

"Mark told me," Pamela said. "Are you okay?"

"I don't know yet."

"So, what are you two talking about?" Connie aske when she returned to the living room.

"I was just asking how Jack was doing," Pamela answered.

"He sounded like he was doing better, but after you left yesterday, he was a wreck."

Cory didn't react. He was tired of talking about Sir and had much more important things on his mind.

"When did everyone finally leave?" Pamela asked.

"They started leaving around three and by five everyone had gone. I helped Stella clean up a bit before I left an hour later."

"That was nice of you."

"There's absolutely no way I would ever help that woman," Cory said.

"Why not?"

"She's nothing but a vulture. Swooping in and taking

over someone else's nest."

"But she's Dad's lady friend."

"Lady is a stretch," Cory quipped.

"Really, Cory, you need to let go of that stuff. It's the past. Leave it and move on," Connie said.

"Next subject," Cory said.

"So, how's your house coming?" Pamela asked.

"Great. I should be able to move in this Wednesday, knock wood."

"That's great. Do you need any help?"

Cory looked at his sister-in-law's stomach. "I think I should be able to handle it. I have hired some movers to help with moving the big stuff from the barn to the house. The other stuff I can manage on my own."

"Well, I'd be willing to help out," Pamela offered.

"Me, too. I can always get a sitter for Byron."

"I'll let you know," Cory said. He glanced at his cell phone again and dropped it back into his pocket.

"Okay, that's the fourth time," Connie said. "What's going on?"

"Nothing. Just habit."

"Checking to see if she called?"

"She?" Pamela asked.

"Yeah, Cory told me he had a girlfriend—an ex-fiancé—in San Francisco."

"You did?" Pamela looked surprised.

"Yeah, it didn't work out so we called it off." Cory answered. "It's a long story and not worth repeating."

"I'll fill you in later," Connie told Pamela. She turned back toward Cory. "So, what's this appointment that is so important?"

"It's nothing," Cory said purposely being evasive.

"Then why can't you cancel or change it to come with us?"

"Well, it's…complicated."

Connie squinted and eyed him. He could tell she wasn't going to give up on this.

"I just can't cancel it," he repeated.

"Fine. You know I'll find out what it's all about eventually."

"That's okay," Cory answered.

"Not to change the subject," Pamela interrupted. "Halloween is in a couple days, would you both like to spend the evening with me handing out candy?"

"Sure. Mark's taking Byron trick or treating so I can come by," Connie said.

"I have no plans so, count me in." Cory agreed.

CHAPTER THIRTEEN

Cory leaned against his rental car staring at the view from the top level of the parking garage on Pill Hill as the locals called the location of the Oregon Health Science University. Portland spread out on the east bank of the Willamette River. In the distance was Mt. Hood, its top covered in snow already. Cory glanced at his cell phone again.

He needed to talk to someone but Luke was away, somewhere over the U.S. working. He thought about calling Pamela but she was at her own appointment and then shopping with Connie. He thought about calling Katherine but how could he talk to her about his appointment when he didn't even tell her there was a problem. He dialed Luke's number to leave him a message.

"Hello."

"Luke?"

"Cory?"

"I thought you'd be working."

"We just landed."

"You're back in town?"

"Yes. Why? Is everything okay? You sound worried."

"Can we meet up? I really need to talk to someone."

"Sure. It'll take me an hour to get home. I live in the Pearl. You wanna come by?"

"That would be great."

An hour later Cory stood outside the front door of Luke's condo. He was nervous. He knocked on the door. It opened right away as though Luke were waiting on the other side.

"Come in," Luke invited.

The apartment smelled of cinnamon and spice. A welcoming scent that brought back memories of holiday baking.

"How have you been?" Luke asked and gave Cory a hug.

Cory hesitated then hugged him back.

"You're trembling," Luke said while he stepped back. "What's the matter?"

"I had an appointment at the Oregon Health Science University."

"Come in and sit down."

Luke led Cory into down a small hall to the open concept living, dining and kitchen. The windows on the outer wall provided a view of the neighboring high-rise and a sliver of the waterfront. Luke turned on the gas fireplace in the corner to take the chill off the room. A white sofa with a large pillow back sat facing the windows and fireplace. Cory sat down. Luke moved a magazine and sat down at the opposite end.

"Now, what did the doctor say?"

"He told me he's done this procedure many times. He's very optimistic he can fix my aorta and with blood pressure meds, I shouldn't have any more trouble."

"Well, that's great!" Luke said and nodded. "Isn't it?"

"I guess so," Cory agreed with less enthusiasm.

"But…"

"Since the weak spot is near my heart they classify it as major surgery. They'll have to cut into my chest. That thought alone terrifies me."

"Well, I've heard the surgeons at OHSU are the best." Luke said. "You'll be okay."

Cory looked at him and then looked away.

"I think you need a drink. Would you like a Coke?"

"Sure."

While Luke went to get the drinks, Cory stared at the flames in the fireplace. He wasn't thinking about anything specifically. He let his mind rest.

"Here you go," Luke said when he returned with their drinks. He sat down a bit closer to Cory so their shoulders nearly touched.

"Thank you," Cory said before taking a sip of his drink.

"So, when you look at your life," Luke said. "Has it turned out as you envisioned it would?"

"Where did that come from?" Cory asked and pulled away so he could look at the man beside him.

Luke laughed. "Just curious."

Cory settled back and let his shoulder touch Luke's. "Not really," he answered. "Before my mom died, I always dreamed of being Robin to my friend Paul's Batman. That aint happening." Cory laughed which made Luke smile. "Later, in high school, I wanted to be an English teacher."

"Why? Did you have a good English teacher or something?"

"Yeah. Mr. Stephanopoulos. He had a certain classiness about him and not just because he always wore a shirt and tie and a blazer with his jeans. He spoke really well. I wanted to be like him."

"I see. So, is that why you wear that blazer now?"

Cory looked down and then looked at Luke. "I never really thought about it, but maybe.

"So, how about you? Did life turn out like you wanted?"

"Wow!" Luke said and looked surprised. "You know, no one has ever asked me that question. I'm usually the one that asks. It's a sort of icebreaker."

"So…?"

"I guess I would say, for the most part it has. I mean, ever since my first time flying when I was a kid, I wanted to be a flight attendant. In high school I was worried when I started to get taller because I always heard there is a maximum height cut off. But when I actually applied I found out there wasn't any restrictions."

"What about your home life?"

"What about yours?"

"No fair," Cory laughed again. "I asked you first."

"Fine. The only piece missing in my life is having

someone to come home to. I always wanted that someone special but with my work schedule I'm in the air most of the time and away a lot. Not too conducive to maintaining any sort of relationship."

"I get that. I don't want to be alone. I remember when I was a kid, there was an old man down the street. I'd see him working in his yard but never talking to anyone or having any company stop by. I felt sad for him. Then one day he wasn't there anymore. I noticed a strange car in his driveway and I asked the woman who came out of his house what happened to him. She said he died in his sleep. I don't want to end up like him."

"Wow," Luke breathed. "That is awful."

The both took a sip of their drinks at the same time while they continued to stare at the fire.

CHAPTER FOURTEEN

"So where have you been?" Connie snapped and pushed her way into the motel room passed Cory.

"Well, good morning to you, too," Cory said with a yawn. He dug his hands into the pockets of his terrycloth bathrobe and walked back to the bathroom, leaving is sister to close the door.

"You haven't answered my question," Connie called.

"I was out," Cory answered. He folded his bathrobe up and set it on the counter before buttoning up his jeans. He pulled his blue sweater over his plaid shirt. Taking his robe, he emerged from the bathroom. He put his robe in the suitcase that lay open on the neatly made bed.

"Out? I haven't been able to reach you for two days!" Connie persisted. She folded her arms over her chest. "You were supposed to spend Halloween with Pamela and me, did you forget?"

Cory finished tying his shoelaces and sat up. He looked

at his sister and a vision of his mother flashed in his mind. He had never thought about how much Connie looked like her until that moment.

"I'm sorry." he said, trying not to sound too annoyed, even though he was. He stood up and walked over to the dresser.

"I'm sorry? Cory, I was trying to reach you and I was getting worried." Her tone softened and became more like his sister's and less like their mother's.

Cory took his toiletry bag and packed it in his suitcase. "I had a lot on my mind. I just needed time to think."

"Is it due to that appointment thing you had the other day?" She sat down in the chair beside the small table.

"Partly. Stop with the questions already." Cory went to retrieve the last of this things from the closet.

"Just where was this appointment?"

"I told you already."

"You said 'in Portland,' what I want to know is where?" Connie looked at her brother curiously.

"Will you just drop it?"

"No. There's something wrong. I just know it."

"Wrong? Why does my having an appointment mean something's wrong?"

"Because ever since you've been back you have been acting strange."

"I have?" Cory was becoming uncomfortable with the direction of the conversation. "I just have a lot on my mind with the house delays, Kyle, the funeral, seeing Sir again, it's all a bit much for me to take in."

Cory could tell by the look on his sister's face that she

wasn't buying his story.

"What's really going on, Cory?" she asked. "What are you trying so hard not to tell me? Are you having second thoughts about breaking up with Katherine—"

"No!" Cory snapped. "I just took a drive, for god's sake. That is all. No big secret."

"It's that flight attendant isn't it? I should never have called him."

"Why would you say that?"

"I saw the way he looked at you in the airport—"

"Connie! Enough already! Just drop it!" Cory snapped angrily.

Connie recoiled sharply, as though she had been slapped. "Forgive me if I'm a little worried about you. I haven't seen you in years and I'm just afraid of losing you again."

"You aren't going to lose me," Cory answered in a gentler tone. "I'm fine, really. I'm not going anywhere, not in a million years." He kissed her forehead and smiled before returning to his packing. "So, how did shopping with Pam after her check up?" Cory changed the subject.

"It went okay." Connie answered but sounded a bit disconnected. She wasn't her usual cheery self. "It would have been more fun if you were there."

"So, what's she having? Did the doctor tell her?"

"Yeah, but she wants to tell you."

"Come on. Tell me. I'll still pretend to be surprised."

"You're an author, not an actor. Besides, I promised her I wouldn't ruin her surprise. You're not the only one who can keep secrets."

Cory glared at her.

"Oh, get this!" Connie said. "Her doctor moved her due date up. It's now Christmas Day."

"You're joking."

"No, that's what she said. Wouldn't that be wonderful? Talk about the perfect present. A Christmas baby. When we were shopping I found the cutest little sleeper. It's a red and white onesie Santa suit with matching hat." She started talking very fast. Ever since she was a little girl, whenever she would get excited she would rattle on in machine gun speed. Cory found it difficult to keep up with her and only heard half of what she said.

"What else did you find at the mall?"

"Pam picked up several onesies. I told her when I had Byron I was constantly running out and having to wash them. So, she bought as many as she could find. We also picked up little booties and sweaters. With a winter baby he's going to need them. Oh, she grabbed several receiving blankets and a couple of those hypoallergenic, thermal blankets."

"So, what's left for me to get?"

"She needs help putting together the crib, dresser and changing table that Kyle bought before…"

Cory didn't hear her. There was a strange feeling in his chest. He staggered and put his hand on the dresser to steady himself. He stared at the floor and took deliberate deep breaths until the feeling subsided.

"What is it? What's the matter?" Connie asked. She put her hand on his shoulder and stooped to look into his eyes.

Cory looked at her.

"What?" Oh, nothing," he said and forced a smile. "Just a little dizzy all of the sudden."

Connie pursed her lips.

"That wasn't nothing," she said.

"I'm fine. Just tired. I'm checking out of here today and finally moving into my house."

"Oh!" Connie gasped. "Can I come?"

"Not yet. I want everything to be perfect before you guys see it."

"It doesn't matter."

"Please…"

"Fine. I have things to do today anyway. Mark's off and watching Byron so I can get away."

"Good."

CHAPTER FIFTEEN

Cory stood on the front porch of his house and leaned against the column at the top of the steps. He folded his arms over his chest to shield himself from the cold November air. From where he stood he could see down the long gravel driveway to the main road. It had taken him three days with help from a few local college students to get his things moved from the barn into the house and unpacked. Finally he was settled enough to have his first guest. His heart beat fast with nervous anticipation.

He glanced at his watch. "Where are you?" he said out loud. "I hope you didn't get lost." He began to pace. When he looked toward the road, a car was slowly moving up the drive, a small cloud of dust bellowed behind it.

Cory rushed back into the house. He quickly surveyed the living room to be sure everything was in its place. He turned toward the dining room and frowned at the boxes that covered the table. He regretted sleeping in that morning and not getting up to finish unpacking. But, he was too tried and the chance of breaking something was too great.

He took a deep breath and slowly let it out to calm his nerves. Then he walked back through the front door right when the car pulled to a stop.

"I hope you brought an overnight bag," he called when the car door opened.

"I did," Luke answered and removed his sunglasses. "Wow! Why, Mister Martin, this is beautiful, so, rustic."

"Thanks," Cory nodded and reached to take Luke's duffel bag.

"I've got it," Luke said and pulled it away.

The two walked up the two steps to the front porch.

"You have quite the view from here," Luke commented.

"Yes. It's just how I remembered it," Cory agreed and looked at the view again. "The trees are a bit taller but all in all it's the same. My good friend Todd used to live here when we were kids. After his dad died, his mother put the house up for sale about five years ago. I bought it with the thought that one day I might move back or at least hold onto it as an investment."

"Good thinking."

"At night you can see the lights of Forest Grove in the distance."

"Nice," Luke said.

Cory pointed in toward the west end of town. "I grew up over there. Sir still lives there."

"Small world."

"Come on, I'll show you around." Cory opened the front door and let Luke step inside.

"Wow, that's some fireplace," Luke said and leaned his head back while his eyes followed the bricks to the ceiling two stories above them. "Who's the painting of? Is that Katherine?"

Cory looked at the painting that hung on the wall between the fireplace and the front windows. It was a portrait of a young woman with long auburn hair.

"No, that's my mother."

"Pretty."

"She was," Cory agreed. "She died on my twelfth birthday. Cancer."

"I'm sorry."

"I had it painted when I was in San Francisco. He did a good job, I think.

"Come on, there's more to see." Cory turned around. "Over there is the dining room. Please excuse the boxes." As you can see, I still have some unpacking to do, so don't look too long." Cory mounted the stairs between the dining room and living room. "Come with me and I'll show you where you will be sleeping."

"I'm right behind you." Luke smiled.

At the top of the stairs, to the left, was a small loft area that that was open to the living room below. A desk with a computer, complete with printer and scanner, sat against the banister. A bookcase with books neatly arranged spanned the far wall. Two wingback chairs sat on either side of a small side table. A floor lamp sat behind it.

"Nice," Luke commented and continued following

Cory.

"I hope you didn't carry all of that up here by yourself," Luke said in a scolding tone.

"No, I had some college guys help. They did all the lifting. I didn't lift anything heavier than a book. Promise," Cory answered. He stopped outside a door in a short hallway. "Here's the upstairs bathroom and across the hall is the guest bedroom."

"Is that where I'll be staying?"

Cory flipped the light on to reveal a room filled with boxes and a bed frame leaning against the wall.

"This is my bedroom," Cory said and continued to the end of the hall.

The room was set up with a king-sized bed centered on the far wall with matching nightstands on either side. A heavy quilt of hunter green and autumn colored fabrics was draped across the foot of the bed. In the corner to the left of the door sat an antique rocking chair.

"Wow. Who decorated this place?" Luke said almost sounding sarcastic.

Cory ignored him and walked into the room to a door on the right. "I had the bathroom completely redone." He reached in and turned on the light.

Luke peeked into the room. "Wow. That's what I call a man's bathroom. That shower is fantastic. Big enough for a party."

"It's not that big," Cory said and shut the light off.

"So, where am I sleeping?" Luke asked.

Cory looked at the bed. He felt nervous.

"There's another guest room set up downstairs," he

said and started for the door.

"What would you say if I wanted to sleep here?" Luke said. "The bed is big enough."

Cory stopped and turned back. He looked at his bed and then at Luke. He wasn't sure what to say. Deep down he wanted to say yes but he was afraid.

"That's okay, I can sleep downstairs," Luke said. "Go on, show me to my room."

Cory turned around and led the way back downstairs to the guest bedroom in the back of the house across from the kitchen. Luke dropped his bag on the bed.

"This is a really nice place you have here."

"Thanks." Cory answered and felt guilty for not letting Luke stay upstairs. "Want something to drink?"

"I don't suppose you have any beer?"

"As a matter of fact," Cory answered and headed for the kitchen. "I anticipated you might like one so, for the first time, I picked some up at the store. I hope it's to your liking."

"I'm not that picky," Luke said. He followed Cory into the kitchen.

Cory took a brown bottle out of the refrigerator and twisted the cap off. He reached for a glass in the cupboard.

"The bottle is fine," Luke said, stopping him.

When Cory turned around Luke put his arms around him, pinning him against the counter. He leaned in. Cory closed his eyes as their lips met. Cory wrapped his arms around Luke and held on. His knees began to tremble and felt weak. His heart raced in his chest.

Slowly Luke pulled back. He smiled at Cory.

"Are you okay?"

"Yes," Cory answered. "Why don't you take your stuff upstairs. You can sleep with me tonight."

"Really? Are you sure?"

"Yes," Cory answered.

That evening, after dinner, Luke sat on the floor in the living room with his back against the sofa. Cory sat beside him enjoying the warmth from the fire in the fireplace.

"This is nice," Luke said.

Cory glanced at him. "Yes it is. I can't explain it but I really enjoy sitting here with you."

"You do?" Luke turned and looked at Cory. He smiled and put his arm around Cory's shoulders. "I do too."

Cory leaned closer and put his head against Luke's. He closed his eyes and he listened to the sound Luke breathing. It was a slow steady rhythm. He felt his body relax.

Cory didn't know how long he had been asleep. When he woke up he was laying on the sofa, the throw blanket covering him. He was alone. He sat up and looked around the living room. Had he been dreaming, he wondered. Then he saw the two glasses on the coffee table. He stood up and stretched.

"Well, good morning sleepy head," Luke said while he walked out of the kitchen with two cups of hot coffee.

"Morning?" Cory looked out the window. "What time is it?"

"It's about eight."

"Eight!" Cory groaned. "But…"

"We have plenty of time. Let's go out on the porch and sit in the sun."

The two sat quietly on the front porch swing. The morning air was a bit cool, Cory inched closer to Luke. He could feel the warmth of Luke's body and smelled the scent of his cologne. He looked at Luke.

"What?" Luke asked.

"Nothing," Cory answered. "I was just thinking, that's all."

"About what?"

"About how this feels," Cory said. He reached over and touched Luke's soft hair. "I've never felt like this before."

"Like what?"

"Happy. Comfortable."

"So what are you saying?"

"I don't know. Maybe I'm thinking too much," Cory answered. "Remember how I said I broke up with Katherine because it didn't feel right?"

Luke nodded.

"Well, this. You being here and my being with you now; this feels right."

"I see."

"Would it scare you if I told you, I think I could fall in love with you," Cory said.

"Really?" Luke looked at him. "But I thought you weren't gay?"

"Maybe I am," Cory said.

"I need more than a maybe," Luke said.

"I just don't know yet."

"What would it take to be sure?"

Cory felt nervous. He couldn't look at Luke. "I'd like

you to sleep in my bed…with me."

Luke smiled. He leaned closer. "Come on."

Cory let himself be led back into his house and up the stairs to his bedroom. Luke drew him in and their mouths opened to each other. After that, everything was a blur of tangled sheets, sweat, pain and release. Cory had never felt anything like this before, so gentle, so good, so right. He didn't want it to end.

In the afterglow, Cory lay with his head resting on Luke's bare chest. He listened to Luke's heartbeat. It was calming. He closed his eyes. Never in a million years did he imagine he could feel so secure, so content and happy. Making love to Luke felt so different than his previous experiences with a man. It was an emotional connection as well as physical.

Cory raised his head and looked into Luke's blue eyes. He smiled. "I'm sure," he said.

CHAPTER SIXTEEN

The autumn air smelled fresh and clean after the previous night's rainfall. Cory and Luke sat on the front porch and sipped their morning coffee. The sun's warm rays felt good against Cory's face.

"Have you told your family about your surgery yet?" Luke asked.

"No, I haven't."

"Why not?"

"I don't know. I guess I'm just afraid to."

"Afraid of what? You said that you're close with your sister and her husband and your sister-in-law. I'm sure they would be very supportive. What's to be afraid of?"

"I guess I'm just afraid that telling them will make it all too real."

"Cory, it is real. Not telling them isn't going to change that. But telling them will give them a chance to help you, take care of you, be an encouragement."

Cory looked at Luke. "I guess I'm just not used to being taken care of. I've always taken care of everyone else."

"Well, then it's time to let them take care of you for a change. Don't you think?"

"You'll be there with me?"

Luke shook his head. "I think this is something you need to do on your own. Besides, they will wonder who I am and what I'm doing there. It might be too much of a distraction."

Cory thought for a moment. "I suppose you're right."

"Why don't you call them today and invite them over for dinner tonight?" Luke suggested.

"But—"

"But nothing," Luke said. "The house is ready. We've unpacked the rest of the boxes and set up the spare bedroom. No more excuses."

"Fine."

The day passed all too quickly for Cory. After making the phone calls and running into town for groceries, the time had come for Luke to head back to Portland.

"You're going to do just fine," he said, taking Cory's hands in his. "There's no reason to be nervous or afraid. If they love you as much as you say, they will want to be there for you. Let them. I'll only be gone for a few days. I'll be back in time for your surgery, I promise." He kissed Cory's cheek and returned to his packing. "Then I'm going to take some time off so I can take care of you."

"I wish you didn't have to go at all," Cory said. "I wish you could stay."

"I do too," Luke said. He looked across the bed at Cory. "But I have to get back to my job." He put the last of his things into his duffel bag. "You'll be fine," Luke said zipping his bag closed.

Cory shook his head, unable to find his voice and afraid if he did try to speak, he would cry. Never before had he fallen so fast and so hard for anyone.

"Oh, come here," Luke said and put his arms around Cory. "I will be back," he promised and gave him a kiss.

The two walked down the stairs. They kissed again at the front door. Cory wrapped his arms around Luke.

"I don't want to let you go," Cory said with tears in his eyes.

"It's okay," Luke assured him. He pulled away to look into Cory's eyes. "I'll call you tonight and let you know where I'm staying." He frowned and wiped a tear from Cory's cheek. He kissed it. "I think I'm falling in love with you, Mr. Martin," he said. "But I have to go or I'll miss my flight. When I call, I want to hear how your evening went."

"Okay," Cory nodded.

Cory stood on the front porch and watched Luke walk down the steps and around the front of his car. Luke opened the back door and threw his duffel bag onto the seat. He paused and looked back at Cory. He winked at him before slipping behind the wheel.

Slowly the car started down the long drive. Cory waved and fought back his tears. His heart leapt when he noticed that Luke's car was stopping. Just then, he noticed another car. It was coming up the drive. Luke had only pulled over to let the other car pass. As the other car drew closer, Cory recognized it. He quickly rushed into the house to the kitchen. He washed his tears away in the sink and dried his face on a hand towel. He returned to the porch just in time to see Connie step out of her car.

"Wasn't that your flight attendant friend? What was his name?" Connie asked while she walked up the front steps .

"Lucas," Cory answered and nodded, "And yes, it was."

"What was he doing here?" She asked and gave him a hug and kiss on the cheek.

"What are you doing here so early?" he asked, avoiding her question.

"I couldn't wait for tonight. I had to stop by and see if there was anything I could do to help."

"No need. I've got it all under control."

"I see," Connie said and glanced over her shoulder at the drive. "So, since I'm here, why don't you show me around."

"Sure."

Cory gave his sister a tour of his house. They returned to the living room.

"The house certainly looks wonderful. No one would ever guess this was once an old neglected, run down house. The contractors did a fantastic job," she complimented while she looked around.

"Yes they did, didn't they," Cory said and smiled proudly. "Would you like some coffee? It's decaf."

"Sure," Connie answered.

"I'll be right back." Cory slipped into the kitchen and took two clean coffee mugs from the cupboard.

"I'd forgotten how beautiful she was."

"What?" Cory asked while he poured the coffee.

"Mom. Your painting. I forgot how beautiful mom was."

"Oh," Cory said while he emerged from the kitchen. He handed a mug to his sister and looked at the portrait of their mother that hung on the living room wall next to the fireplace. "You look just like her, you know."

"I wish," Connie answered. "Ever since I had Bryon I haven't been able fit in my pre-pregnancy jeans. Mom had a wonderful figure after having three. I don't dare."

"Don't be silly," Cory said. "I gave the artist a picture of mom before she had all of us."

"Still, she was beautiful."

"I wonder if all children think their mother is the most beautiful woman on earth?"

"Maybe before they get married," Connie answered. "Or at least they won't let their wives hear them say that."

They shared a laugh.

"I need to check on dinner," Cory said and headed for the kitchen. Connie followed.

"So, how long was your friend here?" she asked.

Cory closed the oven door and gave her a confused look.

"I noticed the dishes in the sink," she said.

"Oh, that," Cory said and glanced at them. "He came out to see the house yesterday. We got to talking and it got late so he spent the night. There's creamer in the fridge if you want some for your coffee."

"Thanks, this is fine," she said, taking a sip. "Since

when do you drink decaf?"

"Oh, I don't know," he answered. "It's been a while I guess. Why?"

"Pam can't have caffeine. Medical reasons," Connie answered.

"Well, I'm not pregnant so you don't have to worry." Connie smiled.

"The house looks amazing. What's upstairs?"

"Just my bedroom, a guest room and my loft office."

"I want to see."

Before Cory could stop her, Connie was out of the kitchen and halfway up the stairs.

"I still have some unpacking to do up there," he called to her while he hurried up the stairs.

"That's okay."

Connie opened the guest bedroom door and looked inside. Cory looked over her shoulder at the bed neatly made and the room looking in order.

"Wow. I can't believe how much you've done in just a few days." Connie said and closed the door. She headed into the master bedroom.

Cory followed her. Silently he wished she'd go back downstairs. A memory flashed in his mind of Sir inspecting his bedroom, tearing his sheets and blanket from the bed. The feeling was the same while he watched Connie walk around the room.

"This is really nice," she commented. She looked at him and smiled. "I'm so glad you are back."

"Me too."

"Oh, one more thing, would you mind if I brought a

guest tonight?" she asked.

"That depends, who is it?"

"I can't tell you, it has to be a surprise."

"It isn't Sir and Stella is it?"

"No," Connie answered and smiled.

"Then sure. I guess."

"Good," Connie answered. She headed for the stairs. "But since we're on the subject of Dad and Stella—"

"I don't recall that we were," Cory interrupted and followed her out the front door onto the porch. He took a few steps and then leaned against the rustic pine post that supported the roof over the porch.

"Okay, so we weren't. Fine, I just wanted to let you know that they had a big fight the other night. Stella moved out of the house."

"She did?" Cory gasped.

"Yes, and don't look so pleased," Connie answered.

"Can't help it," Cory said. "What was the fight about?"

Connie pursed her lips and gave him her typical disapproving mother look. "It was over something you said to her about the house."

His furrowed his brow while he tried to remember what he had said. "What did I say?"

"Don't know, dad wouldn't tell me."

"Is he mad—at me?"

"Funny, no. He actually seems relieved. Anyway, I thought you should know."

"Well, thanks, I guess." Cory said.

"You guess? Cory, I know dad can be an ass at times but aren't you being one now?"

"What?" Cory nearly shouted. "Connie, I've tried for years to get Sir's approval and love, to hear him say I'm proud of you and call me his son. But nothing I did was ever good enough. Forgive me if that makes me an ass."

"You are just like him," Connie snapped.

"What?"

"You are both stubborn as…" She shook her head. "So, what's the story with the house, anyway?"

"Ask Sir."

"I did and he wouldn't tell me."

"I…" Cory tried to figure out a way to answer her that wouldn't break his promise to their mother. "So, what's Sir doing now?"

Connie frowned at him. "I don't know. Why don't you call him? Invite him over for dinner, tonight. He's all alone."

"No!" Cory answered flatly before the words were completely out of her mouth. "Not this time. Not yet," he added. "I want this to be our time."

"Fine," Connie nodded. "But, you know I will never give up until you both have made peace."

Cory looked at his sister and smiled. "I know."

CHAPTER SEVENTEEN

The aroma of garlic, spices and roast beef filled the house. Cory took in a deep breath. He was relieved that Connie had gone to pick up Mark, Byron and her mystery guest. He had just enough time to set the table and shower before the roast came out of the oven.

The water felt good against his neck and shoulders. He leaned his head back and let the water gently cover his face. He thought of Luke, silently wishing he were still there. He couldn't believe how quickly he had fallen for a man and how comfortable he was when they were together. While he dried himself, he thought about Luke's promise to phone later that evening. He took a deep, contented breath.

When he walked into the kitchen the timer on the oven buzzed. Carefully he took the pan from the oven and set it on the cooktop. He slipped the dish of apple crisp into the oven and reset the timer.

The front doorbell chimed causing him to look at the

clock that hung on the wall above the doorway.

"Right on time," he said to himself and took off his apron. He laid it across the back of one of the barstools at the end of the island. He glanced at the dining room table set with his good china and crystal goblets. He didn't know if he was more nervous about sharing his news or having his family in his home for the first time.

"Hi," Pamela said with a smile. She held out a brightly wrapped box.

"What's this?"

"A little house warming gift," she said and stepped into the living room. "Oh, Cory, I love it!" she said while she looked around the room.

"Thank you," Cory smiled proudly.

"Don't shut that door," Connie called as she stepped onto the porch.

"Oh, I'm sorry." Cory pulled the door open again. "Hi, again, sis," he said, giving her a quick hug and kiss on her cheek.

"Dinner smells wonderful," she said, taking a deep breath.

"Hi Mark," Cory greeted his brother-in-law with a hug.

"The place looks amazing," Mark said with an approving nod.

When Cory turned back to the door he froze.

"Kathy?" he said, forcing himself to smile.

"Hi, Cory." She hugged him.

"But? How?" he stammered.

"Connie phoned me."

Cory shot Connie a look that was neither approving

nor disapproving, just confused.

"I looked at your cellphone the other day in your motel room," she explained. "Oops."

"Well, I'm glad you're here." Cory tried to sound sincere.

"It's okay. I don't think she understands we're just friends," she whispered.

"That's my sister for ya. Always the matchmaker. But, I really am happy to see you." This time he sounded genuinely sincere. "So where's Byron?" he asked and looked around.

"He's staying with Dad tonight," Connie answered.

Cory's mouth gaped.

"It's okay. Dad hasn't been drinking and Byron being there will ensure he won't."

"It didn't stop him when we were kids."

"They'll be fine. Dad adores him."

Cory bit his tongue and looked away.

"Can I get anyone anything to drink? I have soda, coffee; I even have a bottle of wine?"

"Wine?" Mark spoke up.

Cory shrugged. "I thought someone might like it."

"I'll have a glass." Mark said.

"I know I shouldn't but a small glass for me," Pamela added, holding her fingers and thumb an inch apart and smiling.

"I'll have some coffee," Connie said. "I assume it's still decaf and not real coffee?"

Cory nodded.

"I'll give you a hand," Katherine said and followed

Cory into the kitchen. "The house is beautiful. You did good."

"Thank you. That really means a lot."

"Connie said something about there being some important news tonight?"

"Really?" he answered and glanced in the direction of the living room. "We'll eat first." He picked up a small serving tray with two cups of coffee and two glasses of wine. Katherine picked up her glass of wine and followed Cory back into the living room.

"That's a beautiful painting of your mother," Pamela said, taking a glass from the tray.

"How did you have it done?" Mark asked.

"Actually, Kathy here introduced me to an artist on the Wharf in San Francisco. I gave him a few old pictures of mom and he painted it."

"He did an excellent job. Nice going, Kathy." Mark said and raised his glass to her.

"He's really an exceptional artist." Katherine said. "I saw the photos he had to work with and I think this is one of his better works."

"Shall we all come into the dining room?" Cory invited.

Dinner went by with the normal idle chatter. Cory glanced at the grandfather clock in the corner of the dining room. The later it became, the more nervous he felt. He wished Luke would call. Just hearing his voice would put him at ease and give him that boost of bravery he desperately needed.

"Here, let me help you with that," Connie said. She

took the meat platter and half-empty bowl of mashed potatoes from the center of the table.

"You guys can go into the living room if you like," Cory suggested. "We can have dessert in there."

Cory didn't wait for a response. He headed to the kitchen with Connie following close behind.

"So, you and Kathy seem to be getting along okay." Connie said while she set the dishes on the island.

"We are still friends."

"I think she would still marry you, if you asked her again."

"Enough Connie." Cory said. "I think we should stay just as we are."

"But why?"

"Because—" Cory stopped himself from saying anything more. "Let's just go have our dessert and coffee with the others." He picked up the tray with plates of steaming hot apple crisp, napkins and forks. "Grab the coffee pot, please."

Connie took the pot and followed him. He could hear her sigh.

As everyone finished their dessert, Cory grew more nervous. He tried to remember the script he had rehearsed in his mind all afternoon, but the words eluded him. He gathered up their empty plates and took them back to the kitchen, his sanctuary, the one room where he was most comfortable. He could think there.

"Is everything okay?" Connie asked when he returned to the living room.

"Actually," he answered, nervously rubbing his hands

together. "That is what I wanted to talk to all of you about," he said, sitting down in his chair beside the fireplace. He looked at their faces and immediately wanted to take back what he had said, but he couldn't. He needed to continue. "There's something you all should know. Something that I had intended on telling you before now, but under the circumstances, Kyle's death, I held off, but I can't any longer. I'm going in for surgery in three days."

"What?" gasped Connie. "What's wrong?"

Cory heard the panic in her voice. He looked at Katherine who was staring at him.

"There's a problem with my heart, more specifically, with an aorta. I have what they call a thoracic aortic aneurysm."

"What's that mean?" Connie sounded panicked.

"It's okay. The doctor at OHSU said he can fix it. I'll be okay."

"What's a thoracic aortic aneurysm?" Pamela asked and looked at him.

"The aorta going into my heart is weak. It happens sometimes." Cory shrugged. "If I don't have this surgery, and it ruptures…"

"When is it?" Mark asked. "We want to be there."

"Yes," Pamela agreed. "All of us." She looked at Connie and then Katherine.

Katherine sat quietly staring at Cory. He watched her clench her teeth and then relax. Her eyes growing angrier.

"How long have you known?" she asked..

"For almost eight months," he answered.

"And when did you buy this place?"

"Six months ago."

Katherine leaned forward and set her coffee cup down. She picked up her purse. "And you're just now telling me? Telling us?"

"Yes." Cory nodded.

She stood up. "I'm really sorry this is happening to you. I hope everything works out. Thank you for the lovely dinner." She headed for the door. "I need some air. I'll wait outside." she said.

"Kathy, wait!" Cory jumping to his feet.

Katherine continued out the door seemingly ignoring him.

Cory hesitated, looking at Connie, Mark and Pamela.

"Go after her," Connie urged.

"We're fine. Go," Pamela added.

Cory rushed out the front door. He searched the darkness for Katherine. When his eyes adjusted to the light from the fading sky, he spotted her leaning against a fence post on the other side of the gravel driveway. Her back toward him. Slowly he walked over to her.

"Kathy, are you okay?"

"No, I'm not okay," she snapped, keeping her back to him. "You never trusted me, did you? I could forgive the lies, the pretend family. I understand you had a rough childhood. But why couldn't you trust me enough to tell me? You bought this place five months before you…"

"Kathy, please, it's not like that."

"Oh, I'm wrong again," she said sarcastically.

"Kathy, let me explain—"

"No! I've heard enough of your explanations. This

isn't all about you. I'm here. I'm a person too. I have feelings. No, I've had enough. I'm done."

"I'm sorry. I didn't mean to imply that it was all about me. It's just that for years when I was growing up I've been the one who took care of everyone. It's hard for me to ask for help and let someone take care of me."

Katherine turned around so quickly it startled Cory and caused him to take a step back.

"Is that what you are asking now? You want me to take care of you?"

"No," Cory answered.

"Good, because I'm not staying. I'm leaving as soon as I can change my flight. This was a huge mistake. Why did I listen to your sister?" Katherine start toward the barn.

"Kathy—"

She stopped and turned back toward him.

"I'm through, Cory Martin. It's over. Finished. We're not friends. Friends trust each other."

"But—"

"Just go. Leave me alone." Katherine turned away.

Even in the darkness, Cory could tell she was crying. He started to reach for her, to comfort her, but stopped himself. He turned around and returned to the house.

When he walked through the front door, Connie jumped back from the window.

"I'm sorry, Cory."

Cory looked at his sister. He was angry with her for meddling. He wanted to yell at her, to let her know how he felt, but his anger dissipated leaving him feeling numb.

"Just leave it alone, Connie."

"I had hoped that—"

"I know. Forget it. I will never happen."

"But—"

"You should go check on her. She may want to go back to wherever she's staying."

Connie looked at Cory. Their eyes met and Cory realized what she was not saying.

"Oh my God. You were expecting she'd want to stay here."

"I—"

"Never mind." He reached into his pocket and took out his wallet. "Take her to the Dunes and get her a room. Use this." He handed her enough money to cover the cost.

"Okay," she answered. She kissed Cory on the cheek and then left.

Cory walked over to his chair by the fireplace and sat down. His mind kept replaying Katherine's words.

"Is there anything I can do?" Mark asked.

"What?"

"Will you need a ride to the hospital?"

"No, Luke said he'd take me."

"Luke? Who's he?" Pamela asked giving him a curious look.

Suddenly Cory realized he had slipped.

"A guy I met on my flight back to Portland."

"Oh, Connie told me about him. He's a flight attendant?"

"Yes. We're just friends," Cory said but instantly felt like a Judas. After their weekend together, they were more than friends, at least Cory wanted more. "I'm sorry, but I'm really tired and Kathy is standing outside in the cold. I hate to ask—"

"No, we understand," Mark stood up. "You get some rest and take care of yourself." He shook Cory's hand then pulled him into a hug. "I love you, brother."

"Thank you. Me, too."

Pamela stood up and picked up the coffee cups and saucers. She quickly took them into the kitchen, returning with a bar towel and wiped off the coffee table.

"That's okay, Pam," Cory said, trying to stop her.

"No, I don't mind." She continued to wipe the table.

"Really, you don't have to do that."

"I know," Pamela answered. She stood up and looked at him. "I want to. Let me help you, please."

"Okay," Cory relented.

She gave his cheek a kiss and finished wiping the table. "I'll come by tomorrow morning and help you clean or unpack or whatever you need." She handed him the towel.

"But you're pregnant, you shouldn't be doing this," Cory pleaded.

"Nonsense! I can still help you. Now, not another word."

"Okay." Cory gave her a quick kiss on the cheek. He followed her to the door and watched her make her way to her car. In the distance he could see the lights of Connie's Subaru make their way toward the main road.

CHAPTER EIGHTEEN

Cory glanced at the clock on mantle again. Time felt as if it were creeping alone at a snail's pace. He sipped his hot decaf and set the cup down on the coffee table. He looked at the clock again. Standing up, he began to pace. His whole body felt electrified. His anxiety and nervousness had reached a new high. He paused and forced himself to take several slow, deep breaths.

"Stay calm," Luke's words echoed in Cory's ears.

Cory felt his body relax slightly. He took a quick walk into the kitchen. It was clean. Pamela had helped him reorganize it along with the linen closet, not that they weren't already but she showed him a better way. Luke was going to be surprised.

He walked back into the dining room and glanced at the clock again.

The sound of someone walking up the front steps startled Cory. He rushed to the front door and threw it open.

"You're here! I've missed you so much." Cory wrapped his arms around Luke's neck and greeted him with a kiss. "I didn't hear you drive up."

"I wasn't trying to be quiet," Luke said and smiled.

"I'm so glad you're home."

"Home?"

Cory's anxiety instantly changed to fear as he realized what he had just said. "I mean, I—"

"It's okay," Luke interrupted. "I like the sound of that." He grabbed the handle of his suitcase and wheeled it across the porch. "Hope you don't mind, I came straight from the airport." He said, looking down at his uniform.

"Not at all."

Cory led the way into the house. Luke left his suitcase by the front door.

"Would you like something to drink?" Cory offered.

"Coffee?"

"Coming right up. You hungry?"

"No, I'm good." Luke answered. He followed Cory into the kitchen and sat down on one of the stools by the island. "So, how are you doing?"

"I'm doing okay now that you're here." Cory set a cup of coffee in front of Luke and moved the creamer and sugar bowl closer.

"Anymore news from Katherine?"

"No. Connie said they had a long talk on the way to the airport, but she wouldn't say much more."

"Well, maybe that's for the best. Less stress and all."

"I know but I just wish Connie hadn't brought her up

here."

"What's done is done. You can't change it. You also can't change how another person feels."

"I know, it's just…"

"What?" Luke asked.

"I just don't like it when someone is mad at me," Cory answered.

"She'll either get over it or not, it's out of your control," Luke said.

"True." Cory agreed but didn't like it. "So, how was your flight?"

"Uneventful and boring," Luke answered. "However, all the other attendants wanted to know about this friend I'm taking time off for."

"Why would that be of interest?"

"Because I'm usually the one who covers for everyone else. The proverbial workaholic."

"Oh."

"It really bothered them when I wouldn't tell them anything."

"Why not?"

"I don't know. This is all still new. I didn't want to rush things."

"I see," Cory said. He tried to stifle the growing sense that he had fallen too fast and assumed too much about Luke's feelings. Thoughts of Katherine flashed in his mind. He wondered if this was how she felt.

"Is everything okay?" Luke asked.

Cory looked at him. "Yes. It's wonderful," he answered and gave Luke another kiss.

"I'm really beat. How about I take a shower and take a quick nap?"

"Sure. Want some company?"

"I would love some." Luke grinned.

The two made their way up the stairs to the master bathroom. Between kisses, they helped each other out of their clothes. Cory no longer worried about being seen naked in the daylight. He guided Luke into the shower. The hot water felt good against his skin but Luke's body felt better.

Moments later they were in bed, sheets twisted around them. Luke lay on his back with his eyes closed while Cory kissed his body. A change in Luke's breathing caused Cory to stop and look up. Luke had fallen asleep. Cory pulled the covers up and lay beside his lover. He closed his eyes.

CHAPTER NINETEEN

Cory stepped from the shower as the first rays of the morning sun brightened the bathroom. He glanced up through the skylight. A thought jolted him. The thought that this could be the last sunrise he would ever see. His legs felt weak and he slid down the shower wall until he sat on the wet floor.

"Come on," Luke said while he walked into the bathroom. "We're—Oh my God, are you okay?"

Cory heard the panic in Luke's voice. He looked at Luke and his vision became blurred. He wrapped his arms around him.

"I'm so scared." His voice sounded childlike in his own ears.

"It's going to be okay," Luke said. "I'll be there with you."

"I know but—"

"No buts. You are going to be fine. I promise."

Cory looked into Luke's eyes. He wanted to believe him and the majority of him did, but there was a small part that wished he could be sure.

"In case something happens, my will is in the red file in the loft."

"Fine. But you aren't going to need that for years." Luke kissed him. "Now, come on, get up and let's get you dressed. We don't want to be late."

"Okay," Cory answered.

With Luke's help, Cory was dressed and ready to go in no time. The drive to the Oregon Health Science University Medical Center was quiet. Cory glanced at Luke from the passenger seat. Luke didn't appear worried. He seemed as calm as if they were just headed out for breakfast or a day at Waterfront Park.

After checking in, a nurse led them to a room where Cory changed into a backless hospital gown. He lay down on the bed while Luke stood beside him, holding his hand.

"I'm so happy I met you," Cory said quietly.

"Me too."

"Remember that day when you asked me how I envisioned my life and what I wanted and I told you I didn't know?"

Luke nodded.

"I know, now," Cory answered. "I want the white picket fence, the rope swing in the yard, family, friends, the happily ever after; but most of all, I want someone to share my life with. I want you."

Luke looked surprised. "Is that a proposal?"

"I know we haven't known each other very long—"

"True. And I'm your first gay relationship."

"We're not children or even young adults," Cory said.

"You don't have to remind me," Luke teased. "Cory, are you absolutely sure? I mean, this whole gay thing is new to you."

"Knowing what to call it is new but I've always been and felt this way. I also know it's possible to fall in love and know when it's right. I love you, Lukas Bryant and yes, I want to spend the rest of my life with you."

The shocked look on Luke's face slowly changed to a smile.

"I love you too, Cory Martin, but there's one thing you must do before I can give you an answer," he said.

"What? Name it."

"You have to tell your family you're gay."

"Deal. First thing when I wake up."

"Okay, deal." Luke bent down and gave Cory a kiss.

Cory didn't hear anyone walk into the room. Judging by the kiss, neither did Luke. It wasn't until Connie gasped that Luke stood up.

"There you are," Connie said and walked around to the other side of the bed. She bent down and gave Cory a kiss on his forehead.

"Connie, this is my friend Luke," Cory introduced. He felt his cheeks blush. He knew she had seen them.

Connie's disapproval showed on her face. She seemed to be glaring at Luke.

"Hi, we spoke on the phone a few weeks ago," Luke said and held out his hand to her.

Connie hesitated before she gave it a polite but brief

shake. Before she could speak, Pamela, Mark and Byron walked into the room.

"Hey, guy," Mark smiled. "How're ya' feeling?"

"Nervous," Cory answered. He took a slow deep breath and let it out.

"You'll be just fine," Pamela assured him with a kiss on his cheek. She looked across the bed at Luke. "You must be Cory's friend," she said and held out her hand to him.

"Yes, Luke," he answered with a smile and shook her hand.

"I'm Pam, Cory's sister-in-law. It's nice to meet you."

"I'm Mark, Connie's husband." Mark introduced himself and shook Luke's hand. "And this little guy is Byron." He picked up his son who pretended to be shy and shrank back on Mark's shoulder. "Are you the one Cory said would be looking after him?"

Luke looked at Cory and opened his mouth to speak but was immediately interrupted by a nurse in scrubs.

"Well, I hate to break this up," she said, standing at the foot of the bed. "But we need to get going. You can all wait in the waiting room down the hall and to your right."

"Oh god," Cory gasped. There was a look of fear in his eyes. He grabbed Luke's hand and held it tightly.

"You are going to be fine. Do you hear me?" Luke said, slowly, deliberately and firmly.

Cory nodded.

"I'll be waiting for you. I promise," Luke said and smiled. "Take good care of him," he told the nurse before leaving the room.

CHAPTER TWENTY

Connie practically ran to the waiting room.

"Slow down, it's not a race," Mark said but she didn't respond.

The waiting room was not actually a room. It was more of a lounge area in the front lobby. Chairs were grouped around large block coffee tables. A baby grand piano sat in a corner opposite the reception desk where an elderly volunteer sat looking over her logbook. Connie gave the woman Cory's name and her name before claiming a seat in the grouping farthest away from the piano.

"What's the matter, now?" Mark asked in a whisper when he sat down in the chair beside his wife.

"Nothing."

"Oh, I know that look, Connie. Something's up. What is it?"

"What do we know of this Luke guy?" she asked.

"He's Cory's friend. Why?" Mark shrugged and shifted

Byron to his other arm.

"Doesn't he strike you as a bit odd? I mean, I know what they say about male flight attendants," Connie said.

"Don't start," Mark warned. "Not today."

"I'm not intending on starting anything," Connie responded. "I just want to find out more about this guy. That's all."

"Connie, I mean it." Mark's tone became very serious and stern. "Today is not the day. I'm telling you, butt out."

"That's easy for you to say but you didn't see what I did."

"See what?" Pamela asked when she sat down across from the two of them.

Connie looked at her sister-in-law and then noticed Luke in the distance. He was headed for a gift shop across the open hallway. She glanced at Mark and then turned back to Pamela.

"When I walked into the room, they were kissing," she answered.

"They were?" Pamela looked surprised.

"Okay, that's enough," Mark said sounding angry. "Don't you think you've meddled enough with bringing Katherine up here?"

"I wasn't meddling. I was trying to help Cory patch things up—"

"And how well did that work out?" Mark cut her off. "I mean it, Constance, butt out. Let Cory live his life the way he chooses."

"But—"

"But nothing." Mark cut her off again. "Honestly, I am

surprised that you didn't know he was gay a long time ago. I mean, I knew it the first time I met the man."

Connie looked at her husband, her mouth open.

"Oh don't look so shocked. I for one am glad Cory finally met someone."

"Wow. That's really forward-thinking of you, Mark," Pamela spoke up. "I mean, not many straight men would be so understanding."

"What's so hard to understand? We are all basically looking for the same thing, to love and be loved."

"But I want—"

"Honey, it's not about what you want. Just be happy he found someone."

Connie looked back at the gift shop. "I'll be right back," she said and jumped up.

"Where are you going?" Mark asked in a fatherly tone.

"To look around. Don't worry," she answered and made a beeline for the gift shop door.

The shop was small. Trinkets and souvenirs lined the outer walls. The wall to the left of the door was taken up by a long counter crowed with candy bars, mints and boxes of chocolates. On the wall behind the counter were displayed various Mylar balloons with silly sayings on them. A single aisle ran the length of the shop parallel to the counter. Connie spotted Luke at the card display.

"So, Cory's gay?" she said quietly as though she were in a library.

Luke looked up from reading a card. "You'll have to ask him about that."

"Come on, I saw you two kissing. Straight guys don't

kiss each other, not like that."

"It's not my place to out someone."

"Well, I'm glad my brother found someone."

"Really? You didn't seem too happy back in the room." He slipped the card back into the rack and continued to turn the display rack while he searched for a card.

"I was just caught off guard, that's all. I had no idea Cory was gay."

Luke glanced at her.

"He's my brother. When we were raised, we didn't talk about sex. Hell, Cory still thinks I was a virgin when I married Mark. Anyway, if I'm totally honest, I suspected he might be but I wasn't sure. I don't dare ask him."

"Well, the cat's out of the bag now, don't you think?"

Connie laughed. "Yeah, I guess so."

"So are you good with it?"

"I don't know. Maybe. It will take some time to get used to, I suppose."

"There you are," Mark whispered while he walked up behind Connie. "I told you to leave him alone."

"I'm not bothering him. We're having a conversation. Can't I even talk to the man?" she asked.

"Yes, but remember where you are. We don't need any drama," Mark warned.

"I'm fine." Connie said sounding disgusted.

Mark looked at Luke.

"No drama here. Just talking. It's okay." Luke said.

"Good," Mark said with a nod. "Come on, we should be in the waiting area in case there's news."

"Fine." Connie said. "You coming?"

"I'll be there in a minute," Luke answered.

The minutes ticked into hours. Every time anyone in scrubs walked by Connie felt her heart beat faster. Flipping through the pages of an old People magazine didn't help. She tossed it onto the coffee table and looked around again.

"How long is this going to take? I thought it was supposed to be two hours," she groaned.

"They'll let us—"

A man in scrubs walked up to the receptionist. The woman pointed in their direction.

"I think they're through." Mark said while the man approached.

Everyone jumped to their feet.

"You're all Mr. Martin's family?"

"Yes," Connie answered.

"The surgery went well. We were able to get in and fix the aneurysm. He's a strong man. He's in recovery right now."

"Oh, thank god," Connie said and hugged Mark.

Pamela grabbed Luke's hand and squeezed it.

"Once he's fully awake, we'll get him into a room where he'll be more comfortable."

"Can we see him?" Connie gasped.

"In a little while, he's still a bit groggy."

"When will he be able to go home?" Pamela asked.

"We'll have to wait and see." He glanced at his watch. "I do need to be going. I'm sure I'll be seeing you all again."

"Thank-you," Luke said as the doctor left the room.

CHAPTER TWENTY-ONE

"It feels so good to be home," Cory said while Luke helped him up the steps of the front porch.

"It'll be nice to actually sleep in a bed," Luke said. The past few nights he spent sleeping on the bench seat in Cory's hospital room. At first the staff objected but Cory insisted. Against their better judgement, the nurses acquiesced to keep Cory calm.

Cory looked at Luke and smiled while they slowly made their way across the porch. "There's something I've been wanting to talk to you about all week."

"Well, let's first get you inside. Then we can talk."

Cory walked into his house and looked around. Everything was just as he had left it. He took a deep breath and looked at the ceiling, trying not to let his tears of relief escape his eyes. He made it. He survived. He turned around and gently wrapped his arms around Luke. He kissed him for the first time in a week, a real kiss.

"Well, guess you're feeling better." Luke said.

"I've been wanting to do that since I woke up."

"Why don't you sit down for a while," Luke said, ushering Cory over to the sofa.

"Will you sit with me?"

"Of course."

Cory slowly sat down on the sofa. Luke sat next to him, putting his arm around Cory's shoulders.

Cory took a deep breath and let it out slowly. "I was thinking…hoping really…if…Well, since you're going to be spending a lot of time here with me, helping me, would you like to move in here, with me? There's plenty of room. We can clear out the spare bedroom. I can get rid of some of my stuff to make more room if necessary." Cory began to talk faster, fearing rejection.

"Well, what are you asking?" Luke looked into Cory's brown eyes. "Are you asking for a nurse? Friend? Or lover, partner?"

"A partner," Cory answered without hesitation. "This can be our house, our home. I want to wake up every day, with you by my side. I never want to be away from you, ever again."

Luke smiled. "I'd love to," he said. "But—"

Cory's smile faded.

"Don't you think there's something you need to do first?"

Cory looked at Luke with confusion in his eyes. "Do?"

"Well, something you need to tell some people," he clarified.

"What do you mean? It's nobody's business what I do

or don't do."

"So does that mean you aren't going to tell your family you're gay?" Luke asked.

"Oh, but I thought you said Connie already knows?" Cory said.

"She suspects. She still needs to hear it from you."

"Why's that so important? I mean, what does that have to do with us?"

"It has a lot," Luke said and took his arm from around Cory's shoulders so he could turn and face him. "Cory, I don't want to live in the closet again. I came out of it years ago. I can't and I won't go back in. Hiding who you are behind lies…I thought you were through with all of that when you moved back here."

"I am," Cory answered. "But—"

"Then you have to tell your family the truth about you, about us. If you can't be honest with yourself and the people you say who matter in your life, then how do we ever stand a chance?" Luke paused seemingly to think. "I'm not saying you have to shout it from the rooftop. Being gay is only a part of what makes you who you are. You don't need to feel ashamed. A very wise friend once told me, if people – and that includes Connie - can't handle it, that is their problem, not yours. At least you're honest and have nothing to hide."

Cory listened. He knew what Luke was saying and he was right, but it didn't make it any easier. Again, he felt as though he was losing control of his life. If he doesn't tell his family, then he risks losing the one person who means everything to him. On the other hand, if he tells them, he risks losing what is left of his family. Suddenly he felt sick in his stomach. He swallowed hard.

"How do I tell them? I mean, what do I say?"

"You'll find the words when the time is right. And I'll be beside you, this time," Luke reassured him. "But you will have to do it. You have to be the one to tell them."

"I love you so much," said Cory with tears in his eyes. "I can't lose you."

"I love you, too." Luke put his arms around Cory and held him. "And you won't."

CHAPTER TWENTY-TWO

Cory appeared to be deep in thought while he set the dining room table with his good china and crystal stemware. Luke stood across the room at the foot of the stairs. Cory looked up and their eyes met.

"Would you like a hand with that?" Luke asked.

"Sure," Cory answered. "I don't think I was this nervous when I broke off my engagement to Katherine."

"Well, this is different," Luke empathized. "You're exposing who you really are to the people care about the most. That makes the stakes even higher. I wish I could say how they will take it but I can't know for certain. Maybe you could find a way to talk with Pam first, apart from the others. I have a feeling she may be the most understanding. But, no matter what," Luke said, wrapping his arms around Cory's waist. "I am going to be here. You aren't going to lose me."

"Thanks," Cory said and gave Luke a kiss.

"Now, I wasn't sure what to wear," Luke said, holding out his arms and showing off his green and gold plaid, cotton shirt and dark, chocolate brown Dockers. "Do I look okay? Not too casual?"

"You mean, not too gay?" Cory laughed.

"Yeah," Luke nodded. "I didn't want to be too obvious, this is the first time I'm meeting your step-father."

"You look fine," Cory reassured him.

A knock on the front door caused Cory to jump and take a step away from Luke. Suddenly the butterflies began to stir and the nauseated feeling in the pit of his stomach returned. Cory stood frozen and just stared at the front door, unable to move a muscle.

"You're going to be fine," Luke reassured him. "Deep breath and let it out slowly."

Cory did as instructed before opening the door.

"Pam!" he smiled, relieved that it was her and that she was early.

"You sure look as though you're feeling better," she said, greeting him with a kiss on his cheek. "I see I'm the first to arrive," she said, giving Luke a nod. "Hello again." She walked over to him and gave him a hug. "It's good to see you."

"Nice to see you, too," Luke said.

Cory quickly closed the front door. "Can I get you something to drink?" he asked.

"A glass of ice water would be fine," she answered.

"I'll get it for you," Luke offered. "That way the two of you can talk before the others arrive."

Cory nodded at Luke's not-so-subtle hint.

Cory ushered Pam into the living room to a chair. "I figure this will be the most comfortable seat."

"Trust me, at this point, no chair is comfortable." Pam sat down slowly. "Two weeks to go and then this one will be out."

"I can't wait to meet him."

Pamela smiled and ran her hand over her stomach.

"Before the others get here, there is something I want to tell you," Cory said and sat down on the corner of the coffee table to face her.

"Okay, what is it?"

"Where do I begin?" he said suddenly at a loss for words.

"Why not just spit it out?"

"Okay." He took a deep breath again and let it out. "I want you to know that I love you so much. And what I have to say doesn't change that."

"You're not proposing to me are you?" she interrupted.

"Proposing? No. I'm gay," Cory said before he realized it.

Pamela laughed and shook her head. "Is that it?" she said.

"Yes," Cory answered, not sure how to take her reaction.

"Well, I want you to know something. All Kyle and I have ever wanted was for you to be happy. We both—" she paused and cocked her head for a second then looked back at Cory. "I love you, no matter what. You're not only my brother-in-law, but also my friend. I'm here for you."

Cory smiled. "Thank you." He gave her a hug.

"Here you go," Luke said while he walked over to them. "I put a slice of lemon in it for a little flavor."

"Thank you," Pamela said and took the glass.

A knock at the door caused Cory to jump to his feet. With renewed confidence, he went to answer it.

"Hi," Connie greeted when the door opened before her.

"Come in."

"Happy two weeks before Christmas," Mark greeted, handing Cory a wine bottle.

Cory looked at it curiously.

"It's sparkling cider, actually," Mark added with a smile.

"Sounds good." Cory sighed, relieved.

"Dad wanted me to tell you he's sorry but he can't make it," Connie informed him.

"Did he say why?"

"No. Just to tell you."

"Okay." Cory shrugged; he was actually surprised that he felt disappointed. "Can I get you something to drink? Coffee? Sparkling cider?" he offered, holding up the bottle.

"I'll take some cider," Mark spoke up.

"Me, too," Connie answered. She froze when she noticed Luke.

"I know what you want," Cory cooed playfully at Byron. "How about some chocolate milk?"

"Ah-h," he answered, pretending to think. "Yeah!" He grinned.

"Coming right up." Cory started to turn around.

"I'll get that for you. Why don't you stay here and visit with your family?" Luke offered, taking the bottle of cider from Cory.

"Are you sure?"

"Yes." Luke nodded. "Hey, Byron, let's get you some chocolate milk." He held out his hand to Byron. Byron immediately took it and the two walked into the kitchen.

"So, what's Luke doing here?" Connie asked while she sat down on the sofa beside her husband.

"I invited him," Cory answered. "Actually, I'm glad that Sir isn't here. There's something I want to talk to you both about." He sat down in the chair beside the fireplace.

"Now what?" Connie asked, sitting forward and looking concerned. "I thought they said everything was okay with your heart after the surgery. You're okay aren't you?"

"Connie, I'm fine. It's not that," Cory reassured her with a smile. "You once asked me why things didn't work out between Katherine and me. Well, at first, I didn't know myself. I just knew that it didn't feel right. Now, I know why."

"Oh, that," Connie sat back.

"I know you already suspect but I need to say it, for me," he said. "I am gay."

The room fell into deafening silence. Time seemed as if it had stopped. Cory looked at his sister to get her reaction. There was none.

"Are you okay?" he asked. He glanced at Mark.

"I know it took a lot for you to tell us," Mark spoke up. "Thank you. I want you to know it doesn't change a thing. We both still love and respect you."

"Thank you for that, Mark. Connie?"

Connie suddenly stood up.

"I need to get some air," she said and walked out the front door.

"Constance!" Mark snapped angrily.

"It's okay. I'll go." Cory stood up and went after her.

The late autumn air was more than a bit chilly. It smelled of snow. Cory pulled the collar of his shirt tighter around his neck. He walked across the driveway to where Connie stood by the wooden fence. A feeling of deja vu came over him. It was the same spot where he and Katherine had said their good-byes.

"Is everything okay?"

Connie turned and looked at him. "I don't know."

"Does my being gay bother you?"

She shook her head. "No."

"Then what's the matter?"

"I can't help but wonder if this has to do with Dad."

"Why would you think that?" Cory asked.

"I don't know. I've heard that boys who don't get attention from their fathers seek it from other men. Maybe if he'd have shown—"

"Connie, stop. That's crazy. I mean, in my case that is not true. I now see that I've always been attracted to men even before mom died. Sir had nothing to do with it."

"That's another thing, why can't you call him dad? Is there something you're not telling me?"

A sudden jolt, like a bolt of lightning, shot through Cory's body. He looked at his sister and the words of their mother echoed in his ears: "Don't tell Connie."

"I already told you I talked to Dad and he said he never asked you to call him that. So, why?"

Cory thought about the day before his mother died and running into Jack in the hall. Could he have misunderstood what Jack said? Could he be the reason Jack seemed so distant? Cory looked at his sister.

"I must have misunderstood him."

"Another thing, do you know why Stella suddenly left him?" Connie asked.

"That I don't know. Did you ask S-s—Dad?"

"Yes, he said he threw her out but I want to know why after all these years?"

"I honestly don't know."

"Damn it, Cory. I'm tired of all these secrets. It just feels like my family is slipping away, becoming strangers to me."

"Connie," Cory spoke softly, putting his hands on her shoulders and looking into her brown eyes. "I'm still the same person I've always been and I am not going anywhere."

Connie looked at him. Slowly the lines on her forehead disappeared. She even managed a weak smile.

"So, is Luke more than just a friend?"

Cory nodded. "Yes. I love him in a way I've never loved anyone before; in a way I could never love Katherine. He makes me feel so good about being me."

Connie nodded and looked out at the sunlight fields. "So, do you think you two will get married now that it's legal for gays to marry?" she asked.

"I don't know yet. I've asked him to move in with me."

"Oh," Connie said. She smiled to herself. "You know, I can't remember ever seeing this happy."

"I am. For the first time in a very long time, since mama died really, I am truly at peace with myself and happy with my life. No more pretending. No more lies. I've found myself. And I like me."

A tear came to Connie's eyes. She wiped them away and wrapped her arms around Cory's neck. "I love you so much," she whispered into his ear.

CHAPTER TWENTY-THREE

Two days before the official start of winter, a cold front descended on the countryside dumping three inches of snow. Cory had forgotten how beautiful and exciting it was to watch it snow. A memory from his childhood flashed in his mind. Lunch recess was over. He was sitting at his desk listening to his sixth grade teacher read a lesson from a textbook. He was finding it hard to concentrate and was nearly falling asleep. The room came alive and filled with ooh's and awes. Cory looked out the large window, at the fluffy white flakes drifting to the ground. It was magical and breathed new energy into him.

Snow still had that effect on Cory. With his scarf wrapped around his neck and his coat zipped up, he shook the snow from the cushions of his front porch chairs. The sound of a car making its way up the driveway broke the silence. He watched the Subaru draw closer and finally stop at the foot of the steps.

"Should you be doing that?" Connie said in a motherly tone.

"What?"

"You know what you were doing. You need to be careful."

"I'm fine. It's been two weeks and the doctor said—"

"I don't care what he said. You need to take it easy. Besides you shouldn't be out here in this cold. Cold weather constricts your blood vessels," she scolded him while she walked up the steps. "Where's Luke? Can't he do that for you?"

"He had a flight today. He'll be home the day after tomorrow," he answered uncertainly. "Either that or the day after that. I can't remember." He turned toward the door. "Would you like some caffeine-free tea?" he offered. "I still can't have regular coffee."

"Sure." She followed him into the house and into the kitchen.

Steam rose from the teacups while Cory slowly poured the hot water into them. He picked up his teaspoon and gently stirred the water until it became the color of weak coffee.

"Do you want sugar?" he asked setting a bowl of sugar cubes down on the kitchen island.

"Sure," Connie nodded and picked up the tiny tongs and looked them over closely. "You're so gay," she teased. "I don't know why I didn't see it before." She dropped a single cube into her cup and began to stir it until it dissolved.

"So, has Dad called you?" she asked and sipped her

tea.

Cory gave her an odd look. "Why would he call me?"

She shrugged. "I was just wondering." She took another sip.

Cory looked at her. He could tell that she was up to something.

"What are you doing?" he asked, accusingly.

"Nothing, honest," she answered. "I just wish you would try to understand him."

"Understand him? It's been two weeks since my operation, he hasn't bothered to call me. I invited him to dinner but he didn't show up. Honestly Connie, I think he needs to make some effort."

"But he's your father," Connie said. "Do you remember when Grandpa Martin was in the hospital just before he died?"

Cory thought for a moment. He nodded. He did remember. He wasn't allowed to go visit him and neither were Connie and Kyle. Jack didn't even go, Cory suddenly remembered.

"Dad hates hospitals. Why do you think he had Mom brought home when it was determined the chemo wasn't working?"

"But I thought—"

"At the time, we all did. But after reflecting on how Dad has acted over the years, I understand him. Did you know when his brother died five years ago, he never went to see him because Uncle Bob was in the hospital. The day he died, Dad got rid of anything that reminded him of Uncle Bob. It was as if Uncle Bob never existed.

"He did the same when Mom died. I remember one night I couldn't sleep and I came downstairs for a drink of water. I heard something in the living room and peeked around the corner. It was Dad. He was crying and tearing pictures from a photo album. Later when I looked at the album, I realized he had torn out all the photos that had mom in them. I think the reason he was so hard on us was because we were constant reminders of Mom that he couldn't get rid of, so he pushed us away.

"I guess what I'm trying to say is, don't be upset that Dad didn't come to the hospital."

"I'm not about that. But he's had two weeks to come see me."

"Have you invited him, not to dinner, but just to come over and see the place? I know he's not perfect. God knows you felt the brunt of his grief the most, but maybe taking a step back and looking at it from his perspective might make it a bit easier to forgive him?"

Cory thought for a moment. "I don't know if I can," Cory finally answered.

CHAPTER TWENTY-FOUR

The knock on the front door was faint. So faint that Cory wasn't sure he heard it. He stuck his head out of the kitchen and saw a movement in the small panes of glass in the front door.

"Coming!" he yelled and rushing back into the kitchen dried his damp hands before heading for the door.

His heart skipped a beat when he came face-to-face with Jack standing at his doorstep.

"Uh, hi," he said.

"Hi. Might I come in?" Jack asked. His voice wasn't demanding but polite.

"Sure," Cory answered and stepped back, opening the door wide.

Before closing the door, Cory glanced out at the driveway. The sun was beginning to set but the snow on the ground still made it feel bright.

"You have a nice place here," Jack said.

"Thank you. Why don't you come in and get warm by the fire. Shall I take you coat?"

"No, I think—" Jack stopped and stared at the painting that hung on the wall between the front windows and the fireplace.

In the flickering light of the fire, Cory could see a tear in Jack's eyes. He helped his step-father out of his coat and then hung it on the coatrack by the front door.

"Your mother would have loved to have seen that," Jack said and nodded toward the painting.

Cory looked up at the portrait. It had been nearly thirty-three years since she died, since she'd made her terrible revelation and turned his world upside down.

"So, why are you here? I mean, you've never bothered to come see me before. Why now? Connie didn't send you, did she?"

Jack turned to face Cory. His blue eyes began to tear. Cory stared at his step-father and his heart began to pound in his chest. His breathing became shallow while fear and panic began to grow inside of him.

"What is it? What's wrong?" Cory demanded.

"You had best sit down, son." Jack's words were uncharacteristically soft, compassionate.

"No! Tell me what's going on. Where's Connie?"

"Cory," Jack said. He stepped forward and put his hands gently on Cory's shoulders, keeping him from turning away. Cory looked into Jack's tear-filled eyes. He could see Jack struggling to speak, to get the words to come out. "Your sister is dead."

"No!" Cory screamed and sat straight up in his bed,

suddenly wide awake. Tears clouded his vision.

"Cory, what is it?" Luke asked. He sat up and wrapped his arms around Cory's trembling body.

Cory looked around his bedroom. He felt his the fog lift in his head.

"It was a bad dream," he answered.

"Do you want to talk about it?" Luke asked.

Cory leaned into Luke's arm. "It was the same dream as before. Sir showed up on the doorstep."

"What is it, the third night in a row," Luke asked.

"I guess," Cory answered. "It seems like ever since Connie told me about Sir and how he doesn't deal well with hospitals and death I've been having nightmares."

"Do you think talking to your step-father would help?"

"I don't know. Maybe."

"Well it's about time to get up. What do you say we go downstairs and I get you a nice glass of orange juice while I make breakfast."

"I thought you had to go to work?" Cory asked sitting up on the edge of the bed.

"No," Luke answered. He pulled his bathrobe on and tied it closed before walking into the bathroom. "I traded flights with Scott and I'm taking the day off. I want to spend the day with you."

"Do you know how much I love you?" Cory asked.

Luke walked back into the bedroom, smiling. He bent down and gave Cory a kiss. "I don't know what I'd ever do without you. You're such a handsome man," he whispered, looking into Cory's eyes.

"No, you're the handsome one," Cory said.

"I think you need glasses," Luke said with a laugh.

"No, I don't," Cory said drawing Luke closer and gave him a proper kiss. "I can see perfectly."

Luke smiled. "Let's go downstairs before you start something I'll have to finish."

Cory quickly made the bed. Then went into the bathroom. He brushed his teeth and ran a comb through his hair. Staring at his reflection in the mirror, he frowned at the pink scar on his chest. He felt it. It was still tender but was healing nicely. He headed back into the bedroom, he took his bathrobe from the hook in the back of the bathroom door and slipped it on.

He started for the stairs but stopped in the bedroom doorway. He turned around and walked over to his dresser and opened the top drawer. He pulled an envelope from beneath his folded socks and opened it. His eyes scanned the document. He tucked it back into the envelope and closed the drawer.

The aromas of freshly brewed coffee, hot oatmeal, and toast filled the kitchen. Cory took a deep breath and savored the comforting feeling it gave him.

"Boy, what I wouldn't give for a cup of coffee," he sighed and sat down on a bar stool by the island in the center of the kitchen.

"You know the doctor's orders," Luke smiled. He placed a tall glass of orange juice in front of him.

"I know," Cory groaned and nodded. "But it sure smells good."

"You know, dear man, we don't have to make it every morning if it's too much of a temptation for you." Luke said sympathetically. He set a bowl of oatmeal before Cory.

"No," Cory answered. "I still love the smell of fresh brewed coffee in the morning. It's homey. Besides, you drink it."

"True. So, what's that?" Luke asked and nodded at the envelope on the island.

"It's something I've been meaning to do for a long time."

"For your step-dad?"

"For me," Cory answered. "I need to see a notary. Do you think we can go to town later?"

"Sure."

Later that afternoon, Luke parked the car next to the curb. He looked at Cory who sat quietly beside him. He smiled and put his hand on Cory's knee and gave it a gentle squeeze.

"You know you don't have to do this today." he said.

"I know," Cory answered while he stared at the folder in his hands. "But I need to. I should've done this a long time ago." He looked back at the house.

"Are you sure he's home? It looks pretty quiet."

"Connie said he hasn't left the house in days. So, I'm guessing he's here."

"Do you want me to go with you?"

Cory looked at Luke. "I'd love it if you would, but this is something I need to do on my own."

"Okay," Luke said with a nod. "I'll wait here."

Slowly Cory made his way up the walk and to the front door. He knocked on the door, ignoring the doorbell to his left. The door opened almost immediately.

"Hello, Sir," Cory greeted Jack.

"I thought you might be stopping by," Jack said. "You might as well come in."

Jack stepped aside and let Cory enter. He closed the door and followed him to the living room.

Cory stopped when he reached the archway to the living room. The room was neat and clean. The book, magazines and newspapers that once covered every flat surface were gone as were the book cases. Instead, the painting that hung on the walls when he was a boy were back. He had thought Jack had thrown them out. Cory glanced at the coffee table and saw a copy of his book.

"Are you going to stand here all day?" Jack asked from behind him.

"Sorry," Cory said and walked into the room.

"Would you like some tea? Connie told me you can't have coffee."

"No thank you, Sir."

"Sit," Jack said and motioned toward the sofa.

Cory did as he was told.

"How are you, Sir?" he asked.

"I'm fine. But I understand from your sister that I should be asking you that question. Surgery went well, obviously."

"Yes, Sir." Cory nodded, surprised by Jack's show of concern.

"So when were you going to tell me? Or were you ever?" Jack asked bluntly.

"I don't know. I didn't think you would care."

"Of course I'd care. I've always cared about you."

Cory felt his temper start to stir. He looked at his book on the table in front of him and took a deep breath.

"Connie said she told you so I thought I didn't need to say anything."

"It would have been nice if you had."

Cory looked at his step-father. Jack was clean shaven, his hair was combed and neat, his eyes were clear not bloodshot. There was something strange about him.

"What?" Jack asked.

"Nothing. Sorry."

"No, really, what's the matter?"

"I was going to ask you the same thing."

"Why are you being so nice to me?"

"What do you mean?"

"Don't play innocent," Cory said and heard his voice raise an octave. "I remember what it was like growing up after Mom died."

Jack nodded. "I do, too. Your sister has told me what you said about that."

"I'm not crazy. You were abusive."

"Abusive?" Jack repeated. "Did I ever beat you?"

"You bloodied my lip once."

"I'm sorry. I don't remember that."

"It was on Christmas day, after you broke the stein I made for you. You were playing with the race track you bought Kyle."

"Oh yes," Jack said. "I am sorry about that but you were out of control. I didn't know what to do."

"So you punch me?"

Jack shook his head. "If I had raised my voice to my father the way you did that day to me, my father would have done more than bloody my lip. I just slipped into what I knew, how I was raised. I'm sorry."

"I had to do all the cooking and cleaning…"

"To be honest, I had you cook because I'm no good at it. Your mother taught you how to cook, mine didn't. I know you were young but after your mother died, we all had to fill in the gaps she left. Connie did the laundry. Kyle took care of the yard."

"While you drank and played cards with your buddies."

"No, while I went to work every day to put food on the table and pay the bills."

Cory's head felt as if it were spinning. He heard what Jack was saying but it wasn't lining up with his memories. He was confused.

"Connie said she asked you why I call you Sir, but you told her you never told me. That's a lie." There was a bite to Cory's tone.

"When did I tell you that?"

"The day before Mom died. When you took the pocket watch from me."

"I'm sorry. I don't remember."

"Conveniently."

"No, Cory, I honestly don't remember. I was drinking and drunk a lot back then. I don't remember a whole lot of those days. You're not the only one who lost someone that day. I lost my wife, my partner, the love of my life. I just hope you never have to go through that."

Cory's mind flashed an image of Luke's face. He

thought of losing him and what that would feel like. He couldn't imagine.

"What's that?" Jack asked and pulled Cory out of his thoughts.

Cory looked at the folder in his hands.

"Actually, it's for you." Cory stood up. He reached across the coffee table and handed it to his step-father.

"What's this?"

"I guess you can call it an early Christmas present, or actually, a late one. I should have done this years ago. I don't know why it's taken me so long to think of it, but..."

Jack opened the folder and withdrew the papers. He squinted while he read them. When he neared the end of the documents, his eyes teared and his ears turned red.

"If I'd done this before now, perhaps Stella would still be with you," Cory said.

"Oh, don't kid yourself."

"Why?"

"I've know what she was all along. She was nothing more than a distraction for me."

"Then why did you throw her out?"

"She left because she found some other sap with more to offer, or lose." He looked at the papers again. "Actually, not having this turned out to be a protection."

"Well, I'm glad for that but Mom still shouldn't have done what she did," Cory explained. "Giving me this house was not right."

"But it was your father's house."

"You're my father. At least, the only one I remember and know. I don't remember him or know anything about him."

Jack sat looking at Cory, speechless.

"As far as I'm concerned, this is your house, your home."

"Well, thank you." Jack looked at the papers again.

"I need to be going." Cory broke the silence.

Jack jumped to his feet and followed Cory to the door.

"Is the invitation to stop by, still open?" Jack asked.

"Yes," Cory nodded. "Whenever you like. Take care, Sir."

"Okay."

While Cory walked back to the car, he kept replaying what had just happened over and over in his mind. Jack seemed so different, so nice, so human. He opened the car door and sat down in the passenger seat.

"Well, that took a lot longer than I thought. So, how did it go?" Luke asked.

"Surprisingly well," Cory answered, still confused. He looked back at the front door. "I think Connie was right, he has stopped drinking. He actually looks better. The inside of the house looks better too."

"That's good isn't it?"

"Yeah." Cory nodded. "It is."

CHAPTER TWENTY-FIVE

The grandfather clock in the corner of the dining room chimed ten o'clock. Cory looked up from his computer.

Two hours 'til Christmas.

Christmas had become just another day to Cory. When he moved to San Francisco, he stopped decorating for it and celebrating it all together. It held not magic, no awe.

He looked over the rail at the Christmas tree in front of the living room windows below. If it weren't for Luke insisting on putting it up, Cory wouldn't have bothered.

"It will be different this year," Luke had promised.

"We'll see about that," Cory responded.

Cory yawned and stretched. He had been writing for hours. It seemed that after his conversation with Jack, his writer's block had lifted. He saved the file and backed it up on a thumb drive.

The house was quiet. Luke had already gone to bed and was fast asleep. He said he needed to get up early to put the turkey in the oven before going to pick up Pamela and her sister.

Cory headed downstairs to turn off the lights on the tree. Even though it was artificial, Cory didn't feel comfortable leaving them on while he slept. He looked at the gifts under the tree. They were all wrapped in shiny paper with bows and ribbons. No more comics from the Sunday paper. He silently wished Kyle would have been there to see it.

He glanced at the coffee table. Two boxes of candy canes with a note attached sat on the end nearest the tree. Cory picked it up.

"Please hang these on the tree before coming to bed."

Cory looked up at the loft and shook his head. Luke had tried and tried all afternoon to get Cory to help him decorate the tree. Seems this was his final effort. Cory took the canes from the boxes and began to hang them on the tree. While he did, memories came back to him. Good memories. While Kyle and Sir were upstairs asleep, Connie would carefully hang the tinsel, strand by strand, on the tree. It was Cory's job to hang the candy canes afterward. In the morning, Kyle's eyes would be wide with surprise when he saw the tree. He never knew, as far as Cory knew, that Connie was responsible for the magic.

Once Cory finished hanging the last cane, he started to unplug the lights but stopped. He looked around the room. The mantle was covered in a white fake snow. Ceramic carolers, frozen in mid-song, stood under an old streetlamp in the center. A ceramic snowman in a top hat and scarf sat at one end of the mantle and a holly leaf sleigh candy dish with traditional hard candies, the opposite end. He looked at the coffee table, at the festive holiday centerpiece Luke bought. The center candles were striped like candy canes. It was simple but enough.

The knock on the front door was so faint Cory wasn't sure he actually heard it. He turned around and looked at the front door. Another light knock sent Cory to see who was there. knocking at the front door.

When he opened the door, he froze, suddenly hit by a feeling of deja vu. Standing on the front porch, with the collar of his jacket turned up against the cold night air and his arms full of Christmas presents was Jack.

"What are you doing here?" Cory heard himself ask in surprise.

"Might I come in?" Jack answered.

"Sure," nodded Cory. He stepped aside and opened the door wider. He glanced out at the driveway in front of the house.

"What's wrong?" Jack asked while he stood just inside the front door and looked around.

"Nothing," Cory said. He closed the door.

"I just wanted to stop by before morning and make sure these were under your tree," Jack explained. "Sorry it's late but I just finished wrapping them."

Cory reached for presents but Jack pulled them away. "I'd like to put them under the tree myself, it that's okay?"

"Sure," Cory said and escorted Jack into the living room. He sat down on the chair across from the tree and watched his step-father play Santa.

When Jack was finished he stood up. He glanced at the

portrait on the wall in the corner.

"That's really nice." He sat down on the sofa. "I never realized just how much Connie looks like your mother. Your mother would have loved to have seen that."

"Yeah, I didn't either."

"So, when do I get to meet your friend?" Jack said, glancing up the stairs.

"Sir?"

"Cory, I really wish you'd stop calling me that," Jack said with a slight touch of annoyance in his voice. "I mean, I thought we talked about that."

"What do you want me to call you?" Cory asked.

"Well, how about dad?"

"Dad?" Cory repeated.

"You know, I don't mean to badmouth your mother but what she did by telling you about your birth father wasn't fair. It wasn't fair to you and it wasn't fair to me. When she died, I not only lost her but two of my children as well."

"I never told Connie," Cory said.

"You didn't?" Jack looked surprised.

"No."

"But you two are so close."

"When Mom told me, she told me not to tell Connie. So, I didn't. She doesn't know."

Jack sat back and stared at the fireplace. Cory watched him and felt something strange inside. He felt sorry for his step-father. All these years he was so wrapped up in how the revelation had ruined his life that he never thought about Jack's feelings. It was easier believing Jack hated him.

"What do you know, all this time I thought you told her," Jack said.

"Is that why would couldn't love me like you did them?"

"What do you mean? I love you. You're my son."

The words took Cory by surprise. All he had wanted to hear for years was for Jack to call him his son. Now that he had, Cory felt all his anger evaporate.

"Cory," Jack said. "Not to change the subject but Connie told me about you and your friend. I hope it wasn't my fault."

"Your fault?"

"I'm the one who invited Wes into our home. I know what he did to you. When I saw him coming out of that bathroom that night, his hair wet, I could have killed him. I should have but instead I threw him out. You never mentioned what happened, so I didn't want to bring it up. I figured you'd tell me eventually."

Cory looked at his hands and took a deep breath. "I didn't say anything because I didn't want to disappoint you. I should never have—"

"Cory, you were fifteen. It wasn't your fault."

"It happened again," Cory said.

"What?"

"When I was working at the library. He showed up wanting to talk but instead took me to a motel in Portland."

"That son-of-a-bitch!"

"After he forced himself on me again, he told me that you and he would come there."

"Really?" Jack said, raising an eyebrow. "That sick

delusional bastard.”

“I knew he was lying,” Cory assured him.

“More like he wanted you to keep it quiet and not tell me.” Jack said, shaking his head. “Cory, I'm sorry I wasn’t there for you. Maybe you would have turned out different.”

“It wouldn’t have changed anything, Dad. I figure I was born this way. It just took me longer to figure it out.”

“Are you happy?”

Cory nodded. “Yes, I am.”

“Good. I want you to know, it doesn’t matter to me if you’re gay or straight. All I’ve ever wanted was for you to be happy. I am so very proud of you, son.”

The words caught Cory by surprise. Never in a million years did he think he would hear them. Cory felt tears press against his eyes and his throat begin to tighten.

“Say, it’s late. I have a spare bedroom. Would you like to spend the night and be here in the morning when everyone arrives?”

“I don’t know—”

“Please, Dad,” Cory said.

Jack looked at Cory and nodded. “Okay, I’d like that.”

The two men stood up right when the grandfather clock chimed midnight. Cory opened his arms and wrapped them around his dad. Jack put his arms around his son.

“Merry Christmas,” he said.

Cory closed his eyes and for a moment, he was twelve years old again holding onto his dad feeling safe and loved.

“I love you, dad.”

“I love you, too.”

Cory showed Jack to the spare bedroom and they said

their good nights. Leaving his dad, he walked back into the living room and stopped to look at the lights on the tree. It looked magical. Slowly he turned and headed up the stairs.

ABOUT THE AUTHOR

Author A. M. Huff was born and raised in the Pacific Northwest. At an early age he aspired to be a writer and over the next thirty years, he continued to write with the encouragement of friends and relatives.

After retiring early from his day job, he joined a writers group and started down the path to publication. *Ellensburg* is the first of a series of suspense/thriller novels followed by *Stumptown*. His other works include the coming of age short, *Running*.

For more about A. M. Huff visit his website: amhuff.com

If you've enjoyed this story, please leave a review on Amazon.com or Goodreads.com.